PRIMROSE

& THE WOLF

A Huxley Sisters Paranormal Romance

J. A. Fales

JENNIFER FALES/J.A. FALES

CORONA, CA 92879

AUTHORJFALES@GMAIL.COM | WWW.JENNIFERFALES.COM

PUBLISHER'S NOTE: THIS IS A WORK OF FICTION. NAMES, CHARACTERS, PLACES, AND INCIDENTS ARE A PRODUCT OF THE AUTHOR'S IMAGINATION. LOCALES AND PUBLIC NAMES ARE SOMETIMES USED FOR ATMOSPHERIC PURPOSES. ANY RESEMBLANCE TO ACTUAL PEOPLE, LIVING OR DEAD, OR TO BUSINESSES, COMPANIES, EVENTS, INSTITUTIONS, OR LOCALES IS COMPLETELY COINCIDENTAL.

COVER IMAGES USED W/PERMISSIONS IDS 19930720 ©SAŠAPRIJIĆ|DREAMSTIME.COM 9329241 ©ELENA ANDREEVA|DREAMSTIME.COM

PRIMROSE & THE WOLF/ J. A. FALES. -- 1ST ED.

ISBN: 0-9907791-2-2

ISBN-13: 978-0-9907791-2-4

PRIMROSE & THE WOLF

DEDICATION

To Nathan, who loves me and puts up with all of that evil glaring when I'm trying to write.

TABLE OF CONTENTS

"HAPPINESS OFTEN SNEAKS IN THROUGH A DOOR
YOU DIDN'T KNOW YOU LEFT OPEN."
—JOHN BARRYMORE

Chapter 1
THE WOLF

"Hello, Little Flower."

A husky voice she hadn't heard in centuries nearly sent Primrose Huxley tumbling in a whirlwind of arms, legs, and golden hair from the top of a ladder in Volumes & Vagaries. She closed her eyes and sucked in a deep breath, willing the energy that shuddered and awakened inside of her to halt. The scents of old and new books, with just the slightest hint of magic in the dust from the tallest shelves, enveloped her.

Meditation had taught her that breathing was much more than a function or instinct. It was a bridge between body and mind. The smells—books, dust, and the soft citrus and jasmine of her favorite perfume—served as a reminder of what world she was in and that she was still the one in control. Never again would she allow another being to take that control away from her. Not even him.

Mason Géroux.

The wolf shifter's voice was an engraved invitation to wickedness. From just the sound of it, she remembered the muscles and hard lines of his body all too well. Their time together had been brief, but Mason had stamped her with an indelible memory of his carnal capabilities. If the man had any motto, it was bound to be "satisfaction guaranteed."

If the Universe were fair, men like that—men who lied, and

betrayed so routinely, and could melt the knickers off any given nun—would come with a warning label.

"Goodbye, Big Bad Wolf." She backed down the rungs of the ladder without so much as a twist of her head. Why bother looking? She knew what she was going to see—a flimflamming asshole with a ridiculously handsome face and silver-streaked black hair.

As her feet met the ground, Prim wished that she'd worn a potato sack, or maybe a nice Technicolor MuMu—anything other than her ripped up, second-skin, skinny jeans. She clutched the book her favorite Paradox resident and paying customer had been looking for tightly against her chest. Its weight rose and fell with the defiant beating of a broken heart.

"Is that any way to greet an old friend, Rose?"

"Friend?" she spat the word as he grabbed her wrist, pulling her around to face him. "Try enemy."

"Those are fine words, coming from a thief."

"Moral superiority from you. Really?" She yanked her arm back, ignoring the surge of electricity from his touch. It still took effort to turn from the square-jawed, arrogant face of the man she once thought hung the moon in the sky. "We both know that locket belonged to my family, Mason."

"More than enough time has passed; let bygones be bygones, Rose." He was insistent, weaving through the tall shelves behind her on carefully chosen magical tiles—ones handpicked to ward against evil and negative energies other than her own—that resembled rough cobblestone.

"The name is Primrose."

"It doesn't fit," he said, wanting, so badly, to tempt her again. "You certainly weren't prim or proper with me."

"How *dare* you!" She spun on her heel in the aisle, tremendous power radiating from the palm she slammed against his chest.

"Rose, no! Please, don't do this."

Shifting in public was forbidden and the repercussions dire. No need for him to know nobody in the town of Paradox cared; the bastard *deserved* fear. Panic and pain were apparent in his eyes as they unwillingly bled from brown into bright gold.

"Do you know what's worse than being a disgraced nun, Mason?" she ignored his plea. "One imprisoned for years after being caught with a pretend knight-errant?"

"No," he gritted the response through his teeth.

"What's worse is being a witch posing as that nun, terrified of being dragged from the dungeon and burned for what she was."

"Listen," he begged her, fighting hard to keep control.

"No, Wolf." She flexed her fingers a bit, so they could both feel the emotionless organ beneath all that skin and bone heighten its pace. "It's your turn to listen. It took me forever to escape that place. The coven we called home abandoned my sisters and me because of my brush with the authorities. They threatened to out us, and we were forced to flee. We had to start our lives all over again."

"I'm sorry," Mason responded with a shudder. His ears began to lengthen, and telltale strands of gray and black fur emerged on the back of his hands. "A life depended on that locket, and I had no idea it would be that bad for you."

"Well." Primrose finished the torment just as suddenly as she had begun it. Once a con man, always a con man, but it was her fault, too, for trusting him. "Neither did I—that doesn't change the fact that it *was*."

Her hands trembled from the exertion of reeling in what her anger had unleashed. She played it off, smoothing a lock of long hair behind one ear. He still had no idea, not about the worst of it, and she had no intention of reliving it all again to enlighten a man who meant nothing to her.

"So," she said, "whatever you're here for, don't bother asking. The answer is no."

"I can't accept that, Rose. I need your help with something urgent, call it a favor." He followed behind her, in the direction of the curious hunchbacked crone at the counter. "I need you to find someone for me, and I'm prepared to do you an enormous favor in return."

"No." She kept right on walking. Her days of suffering for him, and over him, were done. "Go away, Mason."

"I can't."

"Go. Away."

"You're not listening," he responded. "I can't."

"Can't, huh?" Primrose turned on him, mid-stride. "What happened? Did you bilk some other unsuspecting witch out of a lifeline? Do you need help disappearing from the planet before she finds you? I would really, *really* love to help you with that."

"I need assistance in finding a woman," Mason said, "one who recently disappeared."

"Who?"

Mason sighed, "She had your grandmother's locket."

"Who is this woman, Mason?"

"My wife."

"*Perfect*," Primrose laughed, a spark of intense energy flinging books off the shelves around them before she could stop it. "You need to go now. Get the hell out of my store before I end up killing you."

"Your sister Hyacinth was seeing a wolf. His name was Preston Coleman, and he was the brother of an Alpha. I understand that Preston disappeared a few years ago. That Alpha is powerful, and he hasn't given up; he has people still digging around, asking questions and looking for answers."

Primrose carefully adjusted the wire-rimmed spectacles that blocked her dimensional perception and hid Hell's calling card. It was a rule: anyone touched by the realm bore red—the manifestations might differ, but never the shade. She had spent centuries hating the bright red circles that rimmed her hazel eyes.

"So you're using Cyn to blackmail me."

"We've already established you wouldn't help me otherwise, sweetheart."

"Do you see that woman, there, at the counter?" Primrose ignored the endearment, nodding her head in the direction of the ogre in human form at the store's reception desk.

The desk was a piece she was particularly proud of, having hunted it down at an auction years ago. She remembered it well from a jazz club in Berlin where she had found a modicum of happiness, despite

4

her life on the run, during the 1920's.

"I do."

"That's Mrs. Grimm, my optometrist." The matriarch had also helped Prim bring more than a hundred years of sleepwalking—and the violence and destruction that came with it—to an end. But Mason didn't need to know that. "She and her grandson have been looking for the first edition of this particular book for the longest time. Luckily, it materialized in my inventory today."

"Materialized?" he asked.

It was as if he hadn't even spoken. "She's also incredibly nosey, so I'm asking you to stay back here while she and I conclude our business. In return, I'll close the shop for lunch and give you an hour of my time to explain why you're so intent on ruining my sister's life."

Mason agreed, allowing her to approach the desk and her client unhindered.

"That's a fine-looking pup you've got following you around, today, Prim." The old woman took the ancient book from her hands with a wink. "Looks like that big stray you've been feeding in the back alley has finally got some decent competition. If I were a few centuries younger myself, I might give you a run for your money."

"The stray's just a cat—if he weren't he'd have introduced himself by now. And trust me, that pup would only bring you misery," Primrose replied, realizing Mrs. Grimm was seeing Mason for the first time. Who had let him past the crossroads into Paradox? "He's nothing but a Loki or Puck in wolf's clothing; all that man knows how to do is take. Don't let the layer of muscles or the handsome face fool you."

"So that's the wolf that got you into all this trouble." The eyes in the wrinkled face staring back at her remained unconvinced. "Are you sure you don't want to give him one last tumble? No one here has room to judge. Let go and live a little for once. I'm not ashamed to tell you I would, child. He's too pretty not to, and regrets will do nothing but gnaw at your bones for as long as you have them."

"I thought that you and your grandson were the ones gnawing at bones," Primrose responded with a squinted eye.

"These days?" The elder Grimm cackled and tapped at the side of her bulbous nose. "Not likely. Maybe his father, my son, but the boy and I, we're fully integrated into a multitude of silly human habits now and much happier that way. We've even gone vegetarian."

"Not me," Primrose replied, wrinkling her nose in distaste at the thought. "I tried it once, but I just couldn't give up the bacon

"From the way that one looks at you, I would say you're his bacon, and he's been waiting quite some time for another bite." Mrs. Grimm nodded in Mason's direction before adding, "Time for me to take my leave, but you always know where to find Reamann and me if we're needed."

"If Mason wants me now, that's his problem." Primrose went with plausible deniability. "I have no desire to be the man's bacon, or his anything else, for that matter; he has a wife. Our past is ancient history, and I fully intend to keep it that way."

"Don't tell me, tell your *heart*, dear." The rough-hewn Grimm matriarch tucked the book under one arm and headed for the front door.

Primrose crossed the warped wooden floorboards denoting the entrance and locked the door with the twist of a key and a muttered protection spell. She flipped the Gone To Lunch sign over in the window with a sigh before turning to look at her modest kingdom of paper and antiques. Volumes & Vagaries was everything. It was her castle, her hermit's hovel, and her last hope for a life in the heart of a ramshackle neighborhood populated with an eclectic mix of humans and Grays.

The Gray was the name that the outcast Fae, unfit for the Seelie Court yet no longer dark enough to abide by the Unseelie Ways, had chosen for themselves. Primrose had found a wonderful solace in their midst—and a family that would never betray her. These creatures had claimed her as one of their own and loved her unquestioningly, accepting what little of her story, and her pain, she had been willing to share.

Aside from the Grays, all that was left was her bloodline. Her mother, grandmother, etc. were persona non grata, leaving her sisters—Bluebell, Clover, Hyacinth, and Iris—as the only remaining remnants of her old life. They all knew where to find her. One of them must have revealed her whereabouts, betraying her for Mason Géroux. Now that the wolf had shown up on her doorstep, Goddess only knew what else was coming.

Even under the threat of blackmail, Cyn wouldn't have sold her out; Hyacinth knew what it was like to suffer at the hands of a monster. Bluebell had enough complications from her dreams these days. That left Clover and Iris. She would find out which one had done it and determine how she was going to deal with that sister after this business with Mason was over.

"Come with me," Primrose ordered, striding past him.

Mason watched as she waved her left hand over a section of the wall and commanded in Latin "*Ostium Apertum.*" The bricks shimmered and vanished, revealing a stairwell leading to the loft upstairs. Once they were on the other side, she turned and waved her right hand, using the phrase "*Prope Ostium*" to reinstate the barrier.

"I heard everything you said to Mrs. Grimm."

"You're a wolf; I should certainly hope so."

"That was cold," he remarked, after clearing his throat, and followed her up the stairs.

"Your feelings don't concern me."

"Remind me not to piss you off, Rose."

"It's far too late for that," Primrose said as she opened a familiar reclaimed barn door.

The door certainly should have been familiar; it was one that the two of them made love behind a couple of times back in the 12th century. No, she reminded herself, not love—it had only been sex.

Either way, the wood had been resurfaced and stained a lovely shade of cherry. And the rivets had been enchanted to protect her home from everything but Mason Géroux.

"Get in."

Chapter 2
THE SISTERS

"Holy shit, Iris. Please tell us that you're kidding."

"Why?" Iris Huxley dropped the last bite of her caramelized tofu and avocado sushi roll. She glared at the two meat-eaters sitting across from her in the red-padded booth and raised her voice above the trendy music video playing on three out of four flat screens in the place. "Am I the only one concerned that Prim is miserable and going to be an old maid forever?"

The newly green-haired Clover, who refused to eat on principle because the place was vegetarian, nearly spit a mouthful of Japanese beer all over the table. High winds rattled the glass behind her in response, a reminder to tamp her magic down.

"First off, technically speaking, you can't be an old maid when you've looked young for centuries. And second, there's no way he could even *find* Paradox, let alone her place, without one of us. Seriously, holy shit, back me up on this Cyn, Prim is going to kill you."

Hyacinth swallowed another overly chewed mouthful of vegetable tempura dipped in low-sodium soy sauce. She looked around at several immaculately thin, happy couples practically cuddling beneath the muted lighting from the colorful faux paper lanterns. One hand rubbed self-consciously over the fading scar on her neck.

"If it were anyone else," she said, "I might disagree. But we're talking about Mason. The man stole our grandmother's locket and left our

8

sister there to suffer in a dungeon, not to mention all the things that nasty demon did to her afterward."

"I didn't go looking for the guy—besides, that stuff with the demon wasn't his fault." Iris tugged on a lock of red hair. The end changed into flame momentarily as she twirled it around an index finger with a lazy shrug. She was either showing off or feeling guilty; it was probably a little of both. "Come on, Mason couldn't have known about Ipos or what was going to happen to Prim. Even if he did, it's not like we went rushing in to save her, either."

"We didn't rush in because Prim never 'fessed up to what she was doing in the first place," Clover provided a sharp-toned reminder. "And, Iris, what exactly did the undead BFF you want to bang tell Mr. Wolfy Pants when he bellied on up to the bar at the local vampire watering hole?"

"Oh, fine," Iris grumbled. "Just go right ahead; stoop to the usual shanking. You're just damned and determined to rub it in, aren't you? Santino said he could get a message to one of us along with Mason's contact info. Period."

"I may be more determined than some, Sparky, but don't go pulling the damned card. I'm pretty sure we *all* are at this point." Clover used Iris's childhood nickname—from when she'd first started developing her powers and setting fire to everything—and pointed the tip of her bottle across the table at her. "So Santino gets a message to you, and you, being the childish idiot you are, violate the agreement we have with our super-powerful, kind of scary, big sister."

"We won't let her kill you, Iris." Hyacinth set her chopsticks down, determined to stop the sisterly argument that was brewing. When the two had been drinking, even a little, the mixture of their stubborn personalities often proved as volatile as that of their inherent powers, wind and fire. "We'll just have to find a way to fix things. Maybe Bluebell will have an idea."

"We should leave Blue out of this," Iris answered. "She's already expecting a baby, despite the whole deal about our curse-happy maternal unit making it so that none of us could do that. Besides, I'm telling you; Mason is Prim's destiny. It doesn't matter how hard she fights it; he's the one—you know, the man she waited her whole life for."

"Sorry, honey," Clover gave her an exaggerated wave in response, "but you're preaching to the wrong choir on that one. Hello? Lesbian, remember?"

"Person," Iris corrected herself for Clover's benefit. "The person she's been waiting her whole life for—who just happens to have a penis. And I'm betting that it's probably a massive, veiny, throbbing wolf kielbasa."

"A, better, B, you're a pervert, and C, you know I don't care about penises." Clover finished the last of her beer and slapped the bottle onto the table. "And Cyn's right. We're all going to need to put our heads together on this one, just like we did on the last furry problem this family solved. Besides, Blue's insane from all the preggo hormones right now; imagine how pissed she'll be if she finds out we all kept this from her."

"It's still early," Hyacinth agreed, munching on a few of the ice cubes left in her glass. "We can be there in an hour. I'm the only one sticking to water, so one of you can call her, and let me do the driving."

"Deal." Clover threw her hand in the air to signal for the bill. "And quit chewing ice; it's not good for your teeth. If you need water, call for a waiter; better yet, alleviate some of that frustration and call on your powers instead. It's about time you reclaimed them. Forget every vicious lie that idiot ever told you. You're not fat or worthless, Cyn. You are gorgeous; I'd kill to have those curves, so why in the hell are you trying to starve them away?"

"She's right," Iris seconded, scrunching her eyes and holding her hands out as if she were juggling two big watermelons, "the Goddess gave you the kind of boobs skinny bitches want, and porn stars adore. Face it; you're a 1950's pinup girl."

"By the way," noticing Hyacinth's discomfort, Clover changed the subject, "we'll be taking my car. It's less disgusting, and there's more room in the back for a passenger."

"Hey!" Iris took offense although she didn't try defending her filthy vehicular hygiene in any way.

"You do have a lot of junk in the back—old CDs, and granola bars, and water bottles," Hyacinth admitted.

"Honestly, I think we'd all be more comfortable in Clover's car."

"Whatever," Iris said, "but if there is ever a zombie apocalypse, I hope you know, my car will be the only one pre-stocked with rations."

"Rations?" Clover handed her car keys over to Hyacinth. "Don't you mean stale, hippy dippy granola bars and dented water bottles?"

"Judge me all you want," Iris replied. "But while I'm leaving town at a moment's notice with my provisions, you'll be getting your brains eaten out at the local convenience store."

"You know, Cyn," Clover added, rolling her eyes at the "brains eaten out" reference while following the two of them into the parking lot. "You might be wrong. I think maybe we should just let Prim kill her."

"You guys, that's not funny." Hyacinth slipped into the driver's seat and turned the key in the ignition.

"Now, that's where you're wrong," Iris grinned, popping Clover in the back of her head as she slid into the backseat behind her. "When you can't die, it actually is funny."

"Clover," Hyacinth asked as the radio came on full blast, blaring banjo-heavy bluegrass into the car, "would you mind picking another station for us?"

"I second that," Iris said. "How about Metal?"

"I was thinking of something more low-key," Hyacinth answered.

"Please don't say it was Adele—she's the antithesis of Metal; whiny, needy ... forever unrequited."

"Maybe classical music?" Hyacinth didn't bat an eyelash. "Something with piano solos, like Chopin? I saw his first performance in a concert hall—the Salle Pleyel—in the 1800's. I wore one of my favorite dresses; it was light blue with a gathered bodice and long mutton sleeves. A bit itchy, but everything was back then."

"She who drives makes the rules," Clover answered. She made eye contact with Iris in the mirror before searching for channels on the radio. This timid, joyless version of Hyacinth who was always living in the past was hard to accept. It was the kind of thing that made them both wish for a resurrection spell to bring back the wolf that had changed her so they could kill him all over again.

"So, what are we going to tell Blue?" Iris asked. "The absolute truth," Clover answered, unplugging her phone from its charging cable in the center console. "She's pregnant, not simple-minded, and secrets are for outsiders, never for a family."

"I wondered when you girls were going to call," a familiar voice greeted Clover from the opposite end of the phone. "Tell Iris that the baby and I are just fine. We've got lemon and fennel muffins baking in the oven. They will be ready by the time you arrive, so you better have room left for dessert. Oh, and it's fine to go ahead and put me on speaker phone."

"Hello to you, too, Blue. And no, this new psychic thing you've got going on still isn't creepy at all," Clover answered her sister after putting her on speaker.

"Apparently that's what happens when you get knocked up by some weird, dream walking demi-god," the sister whose ties to the bountiful earth had resulted in powerful spells and mad baking skills laughed in reply. "Welcome to premonitions on steroids, kids, and, unfortunately, not all of the darned things are fortuitous these days."

"Nice vocabulary. How's the hunt for the owner of the magical, curse-proof sperm going?"

"So far, the donor-jerk has been unresponsive to attempts at finding him. I may be close to discovering a way to reach him, or someone in his family, though."

"How—did you dig up a psychic or something?"

"Better; I have this friend, Tasha—a retired medium, went into computer programming; for her, it's all interconnected now."

"Tech-weirdo, huh?"

"Not really. She says my sex dream was his construct, a program designed to interact with me. We've almost figured it out. But I'm not going to worry about that until after we deal with the serious negative mojo toward a certain member of this family I have been picking up on."

"It's Prim, isn't it?" Iris asked, gripping the back of Clover's seat. "This is all my fault, Blue."

"Yes and no," Bluebell answered. "It is Prim, but Gran's more to thank for it than you are. I had a vision or a dream, whatever you want to call it. Ipos hasn't given up on our sister, and he just might be crafty enough to follow Mason Géroux, like a trail of breadcrumbs, straight to her door."

"Goddess, this sucks." Iris fidgeted, uncomfortable with the whole idea, in the back seat. "Just when I thought I couldn't get any madder at Gran-Gran, too."

"I know," Blue said, not bothering to point out that Iris still used a nickname from a happier point in their childhood. "And I'm right there with you, but I'm starting to think I've been looking at this the wrong way. What if this isn't just about what Gran did?"

"What do you mean?"

"I'm living proof that the curse Mom put on us has weakened, right? As hard as it is to believe, maybe this is Prim's chance to break the "unlucky in love" part of the Huxley cycle."

"Well, she certainly deserves it," Hyacinth answered. "But how?"

"Yeah, and what's with the following breadcrumbs?" Clover added. "You've never been big on fairy tales, Blue."

"Breadcrumbs and fairy tales are highly appropriate, considering Prim's neighborhood," Bluebell answered. "And I'm not a hundred percent sure on the how part just yet, but I can tell you it's a good thing that Prim is there. My instincts say she's going to need some of those neighbors. Mason, too."

"When you say you're not a hundred percent sure, that at least means you have an idea, right?" Iris asked. "I'll take an idea any day of the week. It's better than nothing."

"It's more of a hunch than an idea just yet, but yes. I need to check on the muffins; we'll talk more when you get here," Bluebell said. "Oh, and slow down a bit, Cyn, or you're going to get a speeding ticket."

Chapter 3
THE WIFE

"What do you mean I can't stay?" Borana was furious with Ipos. "I've wasted centuries for you, Cousin!"

The sweet face of Brunhilde Géroux lengthened and sharpened as the Succubus shook off her disguise. Brown hair morphed into a waterfall of onyx, and her skin reverted from fair to its natural, ruby red complexion.

"Yes, a fact you insist on reminding me of every time we talk." The lion-headed Prince (one of many princes in Hell) couldn't have cared less. "It's no wonder I haven't kept in closer touch."

Ipos pocketed the curious gold locket she handed over without so much as a thank you and smoothed his luxurious, red-tinted mane. He blew a kiss at his reflection in the mirror. Heavily ringed fingers—with silver bands thick as the knuckles beneath them— adjusted his Regency style neckcloth into a crisper bow.

"Don't be so overly dramatic; it's tedious."

"The mission wasn't supposed to last this long."

"Don't worry. My estate's done swimmingly without you—as a matter of fact, this place has thrived in your absence, just as I knew it would. And this whole business with Géroux is nearly done. The plan is coming to fruition; you are going back."

Fruition: That was a new one. He must have invested in a thesaurus for the criminally egotistical in Borana's absence.

"First, you want me to leave Mason. Now, you need me to go

back to him—why?"

"The answer is obvious: He's going to Primrose because he's looking for you. You will resurface while I find her and dis..."

"What do you mean while you find her? Hasn't Mason gone to her?"

"I think so; I haven't had the time to follow up on it yet."

"You said Primrose was your number one priority," Borana frowned at him. Recapturing the witch would get him off her back, but a part of her suddenly hoped he'd just drop the whole thing. Primrose didn't deserve the conniving psychopath; no one did. "What else have you been doing?"

"The opportunity for a little recreational torture came up," Ipos said, waving his hand dismissively. "Members of a disbanded coven following up on an old vendetta. Those poor girls mistook themselves for superheroes; it was too much fun to resist."

"You are such a misogynist."

"It's purely for fun; I assure you—just a way to ease the boredom. And, as I was saying before you so rudely interrupted me, you are going to resurface and distract him. It's much easier for me to bring Primrose back here without the dog's interference."

"I'm a party girl." Borana twitched the red tail extending from her apple-shaped bottom in agitation. "Brunhilde Géroux is a simpering house frau with a nun's wardrobe—not a cocktail dress or mini skirt in sight. Make someone else play the part this time. Preferably someone who might enjoy big, horny shifters jumping out at her from around every corner."

"You're not a girl; you're a carnal demon, Borana. Those infernal pheromones of yours exist for a reason. I had hoped you would embrace the power of seduction like your mother did. You have a duty to improve your skills for the glory of Hell."

"Don't you dare use my mother—or the so-called glory of Hell—against me under this roof!" Borana shouted. "My powers of seduction are top-notch; it's just the penis part that gives me issues. And you're well aware the carnal arts are not my only skills."

She strolled over to a crumbling gothic window frame in

frustration, glancing down into the molten lava moat. A single fin caught her attention. Lovely. Ipos had purchased a fire-resistant shark.

Since falling out of favor with Lucifer, the interior of the ancestral home he had stolen from her, and holed up in, had gone to shit. Meanwhile, the bastard's dogged insistence on ridiculous security upgrades on the outside had made the property a joke.

"My mother retired," Borana reminded him, "because my father was a military genius commanding two legions. I learned a great deal, shadowing Father, as a child. Convince Lucifer to give me an army, as you promised you would in return for all of this, and I will give you all a reason to be proud."

"Genius is generous, and war is out of favor, dear. It's become a crude and tactless human game, spearheaded by silly religious factions and the politically inclined. Frankly, I will never understand the fascination with man-made dogma. No one handed these idiots anything; they carved all their doctrine in concrete themselves."

Borana sighed. She hated it when demons used humankind's absurdity as an argument against militaristic ambitions.

"Besides," he continued, "the idea of a Succubus gathering a legion is utter nonsense! This house would be the laughingstock of Hell. Surely, you knew I would never allow it. I don't need armed forces to restore my position—all I need is one Huxley witch, as a personal battery pack of evil, at my command."

"Fine. Could you, at least, pull your head out of the witch-ass you're so fond of sniffing? Just long enough to realize we're no longer living in the Byzantine Era. My sex life and career choices aren't going to affect your tarnished image."

"Don't be stupid," Ipos scowled back at her. "Lucifer was listening to his advisors and responding to public opinion when he approved of same-sex unions between carnal demons. That was all a political move to further his rule, nothing to do with members of the royal families."

"Royalty *is* politics, and I've done more than enough to further your agenda." Borana paced, the flicking of her tail speeding into a flurry of anger. She paused next to a picture of her parents in formal attire and stared into her mother's eyes. Ipos must have pulled it out of storage just to make a mockery of her homecoming. "I should never have allowed you to take my blood."

"But you did."

"Because I believed you, something else I should never have done; you owe me, you bastard. And you're the one in need of improvement, not me—you're antiquated, laughable, a walking stereotype!"

"I am not a stereotype—and I owe you *nothing!* Without your blood, I would have found another way to create a poison!" Ipos snarled.

It was true; once, long ago, those filthy mongrels had killed someone for whom he cared. Of course, the fact that he had allowed himself to care was something he would never discuss with another soul, living or dead. The rumor of Primrose's secret, and Mason and his pack's proximity to her in France, were the only things that made the wolves a means to an end other than their own death.

"Yes, you are! The way you dress, these cartoonish security measures, and your obsession with one witchy blonde? You're a bad knock-off of Beauty and the Beast—and also a misogynist!"

Ipos paused, waiting for the domestic hobgoblin that limped in with an ornate tray and a binder filled with cloth samples to deposit them, bow, and leave. The tray was chock full of unidentifiable meat, a favorite snack of Ipos's—one more reason for Borana to consider him barbaric.

"I am not a misogynist, per se," he finally responded. "While I can't deny that my time spent torturing Primrose was extremely gratifying, it was done with an explicit purpose in mind. Unlocking all of the beautiful, mysterious power that grandmother of hers stockpiled inside the girl."

"An explicit purpose, how touching." Borana slapped a hand over her heart, watching him open the book and consider a row of swatches in varying shades of dark blue. It had always astounded her that they had anything in common at all, but Ipos's love affair with fabrics rivaled even her own. "Or it would be, if it weren't the same thing you've said about every witch, cursed or otherwise, that you've brought here."

"Never mind the others; I've already told you all that was purely recreational," he said and picked up a slab of something medium rare. "Days of yore, bachelor shenanigans before Primrose Huxley became my bride, etc., end of story. I'll ply her with gowns; she'll extend her forgiveness in time. Or she'll spend the rest of her immortal life locked in a cage. Either way, I win, so who cares?"

Ipos held out the tray. "Care for a snack? He's using apple wood now."

"Are those witch parts?" she asked.

"Maybe."

Borana's lip curled in distaste. Ipos popped something resembling a finger in his mouth and crunched away.

"No, thanks," she responded, "since you can't seem to remember: I've been lacto-ovo-vegetarian for the past century."

"Lacto-what? What does that even mean?" he asked, grabbing several more thin, jointed pieces.

"No meat in my diet but eggs and dairy in moderation are still okay."

"Why would you do that?"

"Why do you think? I've been living among wolves. They rarely eat anything other than meat and their table manners are atrocious."

"If your parents were here to see the kind of demoness you've become, they would be thoroughly disappointed."

"Liar." Borana propped a hand in bad need of a manicure on her hip. "You can drop the *ess*, too. I've already told you: The rest of us aren't living in the past. And your attempt at guilt is laughable."

"So I killed them; they deserved death for allowing you to consider even the possibility of such scandalous life choices in the first place." He waved something disgusting and meaty in her direction. "Look at you; born with that body and yet you rebel against its proper use."

"Why you seriously thought that coercing me to live among a pack of oversexed shifters would flip some hetero switch in my brain is beyond me."

"Have you collected any semen?" He ignored her lesbian pity party. "Like you're supposed to because you are, after all, still a Succubus?"

"No," The infuriated look on his face had always been one of her favorites. "So, whatever demonic date night you lined up for me, call back the Incubus in question and cancel it."

"It's a wonder I bother to dole out your allowance anymore."

"That's my birthright. You should have never gotten your claws on it in the first place—and you know, even now, there are those who will protest if you throw me out on the street."

"Yet, oddly enough, not one has been willing to challenge me on your behalf over anything else." Ipos swallowed down the last few bites before ringing a bell to summon more. "You truly have become a monumental failure—and I never expected much of you to begin with, Borana."

"Please," she snorted, extending both middle fingers in her cousin's direction. "You don't even know the half of it, you stodgy, self-righteous butt barnacle."

"Insolent she-fiend!" he bellowed, raising his eyebrows all the way to his fur-covered horns for even more dramatic effect as the servant returned to swap trays. "Did you just call me a hemorrhoid?"

"If the butt-shoe fits," she answered dryly.

The hobgoblin in the room doubled over, nearly choking in the effort to suppress its laughter. The creature slapped a fresh tray of carnage down, barely managing to escape the back of Ipos's hand as he retrieved the older, empty plate and headed for the door.

Ipos chewed viciously, pieces of meat dripping onto his cravat. He wasn't the type to easily tolerate anything less than a standing ovation for his tyranny.

"By the way, dearest cousin," Borana stuck the knife in and twisted it with gusto, "for once, your fears and paranoia are warranted. Mason's heart always has belonged to someone else; I think he's your witch's one true love. Funny that you practically introduced them, isn't it?"

"Semantics," he said, refusing to acknowledge how deeply it bothered him. Those damned wolves were still determined to take everything from him. He wouldn't let them win this time, not with Primrose.

"Oh, and, FYI, more semantics for you: You can insist on my returning until you're blue in the face. I fully intend to hang out and spend some of that hard-earned allowance on new threads. And, once I'm looking truly fabulous, like the sexy-ass Succubus we both know I am, I'm treating myself to a demonic girl's night out."

Chapter 4
THE TRUTH

Mason sank into one side of a plush, Victorian sofa, amidst hints of lavender and sage. He looked around her living space with careful eyes. Primrose wondered if his sensitive nose had picked up on the scent of fresh fennel over the windows and the doorway. If it had, did he know the herb's significance?

She kicked off her heels, next to his shoes, by the door and walked into the kitchen. Setting a pot to boil for tea, Primrose distributed left over beef cannelloni and garlic bread onto two separate plates and warmed them, one at a time, in the well-used microwave.

It would be rude to make him watch her eat and not offer him any. Besides, she hadn't the heart to do more than nibble most days. It was a shame to see good food go to waste.

The meal in its entirety had been generously given to her, courtesy of an Italian gnome with a passion for cooking. He happily indulged her inexplicable cravings for Greek and Mediterranean dishes after she'd "donated" a book or two on the origins of magic to his granddaughter. The smell of his cooking was often the only thing that gave her any appetite at all.

Mason peeled off the expensive, tailored jacket—one he owned thanks to a chain of legitimate, pack-owned businesses he'd just confessed to—and relaxed into the cabernet-colored cushions. She watched from beneath her lashes as he stretched those muscular legs out and tilted his head.

Light from the window brushed the angles of his face, highlighting his perpetual five o'clock shadow as he admired the exposed beams dotting her ceiling. He had always been such a beautiful thing, like a precious antique or an exceptionally fine piece of art.

"This place—all of it, the loft and the store downstairs—is it yours?" he asked.

"Absolutely." she poured tea with a generous dollop of local honey into a mug for him.

"You have much to be proud of here, Rose."

"I *am* proud, but that doesn't matter. Don't tell me you showed up on my doorstep to play catch-up and stroke my ego, Mason. You need a favor—and I want to know how you found me."

"I can't give up all my secrets, now, can I?" Mason rolled his shoulders back and smiled.

"If you did, it might keep me from accidentally killing the wrong sister," she replied, setting a plate with silverware and a mug on the coffee table in front of him.

"There's that wicked sense of humor I remember."

"I find it sad that you think I'm joking about murder," she shot back, folding one leg underneath her as she sank into the art deco armchair opposite the coffee table. The wood limbs were a rich cherry and the lovingly reupholstered beige and black leopard print cushions were a safe distance from Mason.

"What happened to you, Rose?" he asked, after taking a bite of the food. "This town, the fennel for protection, the witch-power on steroids, all of the hiding and secrecy—none of this is the woman I knew."

"You barely knew me to begin with," she said as she lay her fork down, "and several centuries of life have happened. People change, that's all."

"No, there's more to it than that."

"It doesn't matter. Why question it? You won, after all; remember? *You* got what you wanted, my grandmother's locket, for which I assume you received stellar compensation. And I learned a valuable lesson; that's all there is to the story."

"I don't believe you."

"Said the man who ran the biggest con of his life on me." Primrose pursed her lips, tapping a nail on the arm of her chair. "Who let you into town?"

"A teenager in a red hoodie, with a diamond stud in her nose and some interesting tattoos on her hands. I told her my story; she said she was a sucker for wolves and demanded a kiss for passage."

"Of course, she did." Primrose was going to have to talk with Paradox's council about this. "Riding Hood's no teenager; she's older than both of us and prone to mischief."

Mason grinned, "That explains why she was so disappointed in the kiss—I suspect it was a bit chaste for her tastes."

"Your invitation into my home has a time constraint, and the clock is ticking, Wolf." She ignored the ugly feeling in the pit of her stomach from the image of his lips on Riding Hood. "You'd be better-suited explaining what you need from me, and why you're willing to threaten one of my sisters to get it."

Mason finished the last few bites of his food. She took his empty plate, and her unfinished one, back into the kitchen. The space suddenly seemed too cheery with its shiny silver appliances, yellow cabinets, and teacup-shaped knobs. She felt a sudden desire to destroy every last one.

He remained silent. At this point, Primrose suspected it was a wolf thing, some twisted stab at dominance, forcing her to press him for details. That was okay; Mason could be stubborn all he liked—she would be smarter. The days of her being the first to crack, and the weak one who loved, were long gone. The Truth Tea she had given him, a unique blend, with extra honey to hide its bitter edge, would loosen his tongue soon enough.

"The thing about the locket," he leaned forward, toying with the porcelain handle on his mug, "is that it's what started everything."

"Go on." She scraped the rest of the meat into a small, hand-painted bowl. The remaining dough, which she suspected would be of no interest to the black mouser with the white spot on its chest skulking in the store's back alley, went into a small trashcan beneath the sink.

"I never warned you that I intended to take it, never told you why I needed it so desperately," Mason said as he stood, stretching his legs. He walked over to a large wooden support beam, where a kitchen wall once stood, in his diamond-patterned socks. Closer now, he placed his back against it. "Or explained how my pack mates and I ended up in Anjou because of it, posing as knights."

"It was a wise strategy," she shrugged, closing the cabinet door beneath the sink. "I hardly think that warning me, or telling me some story, would have helped you accomplish your goal."

"Considering the story, it might have—but I wasn't that good of a man, or a wolf, back then." He twisted the gold, crescent-shaped ring signifying pack leadership above the middle knuckle of his right hand. "Afterward, I felt guilty about what I'd done. But my wife, my mate, was very special—and she had fallen victim to sabotage."

"All life is priceless." Primrose fought the urge to throw a plate at his head. So there had already been a woman in his life at the time; at least one, Goddess knew how many more. Why did it have to hurt so much? "One existence rarely bears more weight than the others in the grand scheme of things."

"This one did, Rose," he answered tiredly, "and it wasn't just because I was in love with her."

"Her existence bore so much weight that you slept with me. *Repeatedly*. What a noble fiancé you must have made—an even finer husband, I'm sure." Primrose pointed to his ringless left hand. "Tell me, did this incredible woman still wear a wedding band while you shunned yours and took up whoring?"

"Brunhilde knew what I would have to do to win your confidence. We both agreed a wedding band wouldn't have made sense," he said and continued to twist the Alpha ring, staring back at her. "She told me that as long as she had my heart, the ring would never be important. She's a remarkable woman, Rose—the whole pack, all of us, we love her. "

"Lovely."

"You have to understand. We were dying out from illness; many of us had become sick, and her blood held a cure. Brunhilde gave us back our lives. Someone poisoned her—an act of vengeance for what she had done."

"So the wife with the wonder-blood was poisoned." As far as Prim was concerned, she didn't have to understand *anything* he said. "How does Gran's locket or Anjou fit into all of this?"

"The toxin in Brunhilde's system was supernatural," Mason said. "A demon was responsible, and the only thing that could save her was that locket. We found a witch, by the Vienne River in nearby Chinon, capable of tracking magical items; she sent my men and me to Anjou, to find the one person capable of leading me to it. "

"Me."

"Yes—but, I promise you, once we rescue Brunhilde, we'll find a way to prolong her life without your grandmother's locket. You can finally have it, Rose."

"After all this time? How kind of you." Primrose gripped the edges of the countertop, praying it didn't explode beneath her fingertips. *That* was his monumental favor? She had needed the locket back then, hoped to find a way to undo whatever bargain Gran had made before it was too late.

There was no undoing what had happened to her after he had taken it.

"You were a swindler, Mason—a *fraud*. Why would you, of all people, accept the improbable without so much as a question?"

"Why would I question it? My mate was dying, and it was within my power to save her."

Primrose bent over, laughter bubbling past her lips. Her hysteria echoed through the rafters as she thought of Ipos's last words to her. What he said as he lay there, wounded from a burst of power fueled by her sudden rage—a self-defense mechanism neither of them had expected:

I will find you—you are mine, *witch!*

"I thought you were cunning. Not once, not even for one second did I ever take you for an idiot, and, yet, here you are."

"I have no idea what you're talking about." Mason moved closer. "Rose, what's going on?"

"*Circumdantibus me tuere; dea protege*," she muttered—Surround me and shield me; Goddess protect me—and backed away. She turned, washed the remaining specks of meat from her shaking hands, and reached for a nearby towel. "So this wife of yours disappears with Gran's locket, and, of all the witches in the world, you come to me."

"The witch from Chinon disappeared. You were the only other I could think of to help me find Brunhilde," Mason answered, "and, I won't deny it, I wanted to see you again. I can't explain it, Rose. The connection we had never weakened. I still want you, but I need my wife."

"Of course, you do." Primrose rubbed her forehead. "You had to need her enough to find me."

"You're not making sense."

"Trust me; I'm making a lot more sense than you are. You're not wearing your wedding ring, but you have something else of Brunhilde's on you, right? Something important that she gave you—a token, a picture—what is it?"

"A ribbon," he said and dug in a back pocket for his billfold. "She wore it in her hair when we first met. She asked that I always keep it with me."

"That would be it. Now, shut up and sit down while I gather a few things."

"I will." He reached for her arm. "But you need to explain a few things first."

"No," she responded as she shoved his hand away, "I don't. Take a seat, Mason. You have no idea of the damage you have caused. I need to cleanse that homing device you've been carrying before this pointless visit of yours sends me back to Hell."

Chapter 5
THE BABY

"You poor thing, did you really wake up at 2:30 in the morning with a premonition about Prim?" Hyacinth asked from her seat at the round kitchen table. She plucked a small section from the top of the muffin she'd been given, nibbling at it to stop her stomach's growling.

"It wasn't just that." Bluebell shook her head. A long, black tendril bounced free from behind one ear. She pushed it out of the way and took a sip from the chamomile tea warming her palms. "I have to pee almost every ten seconds now—a full night of sleep is a thing of the past."

"Don't worry; the pressure on your bladder will go away once the little Super Huxley is born," Iris grinned around a gigantic, yellow mouthful of lemon and fennel, "and then you'll have a whole new reason for sleepless nights."

"But," Clover said as she shoved a sharp elbow into her sister's ribs and followed it up with a glare, "you'll have Auntie Iris, and Hyacinth and Clover to count on for babysitting duties so you can catch up on some of that badly needed sleep."

"I'm not so sure about Auntie Iris," Bluebell laughed, wagging a finger in her direction. "I don't want her teaching my baby how to antagonize Mama Blue too early in life. I'd like a little peace in this house before hitting the Huxley troubled teens."

"You know what they say," Iris shot back with a wink, propping both elbows defiantly on the table. "Shit in one hand, and wish in the other, and see what fills up first."

"Language," Hyacinth chided. "You should clean up what comes out of that potty mouth before a poor, defenseless child learns horrible words from you."

"Speaking of troubled teens," Clover interrupted before Iris could bring up her propensity for salty language. She continued, gently choking an extra dollop of honey from a plastic bear into one of Bluebell's prized perennial teacups, "Do we have any idea how the curse is going to work for her yet?"

"No," Bluebell frowned, "although I'm hoping it goes the same way as it did for us. A typical childhood and the aging stops somewhere in her twenties, right before that first hint of relationship trouble hits the fan."

"You better hope so," Iris piped in. "Do you know how much it's going to suck if the terrible twos last a whole decade? Especially if there's no way to kill her."

Bluebell raised her eyebrows, her pale blue eyes narrowing into slits. "No one is attempting to kill my daughter or cracking jokes about killing her; you got it? I already have enough worries about dysfunction from her disappearing dream-dad. Goddess only knows what kind of reception she and I are going to get from his family."

"It could always be worse." Hyacinth patted Bluebell's hand across the table. "Don't forget, you and that baby are two more twigs in the crazy Huxley bundle. Whatever pantheon this guy's ancient ancestors come from, your sisters will be on the receiving end with you. We'll deal with the spirits of the gods and their temperamental lineage together."

"We may be annoying as hell," Iris added, "but we're going to kick ass and show that little girl how to put the fun back in dysfunction!"

"Language!" Clover grinned at her.

"Oh yeah," the fiery redhead shot back, "you're one to talk over there, aren't you, Ms. Holy Shit?

"Alright," Bluebell said and tapped a spoon on the side of her teacup to gather their attention, "enough of the chit-chat, ladies! You didn't come here to talk about your niece or argue with one another. It's time we get down to business. We need to figure out what we've got so far, to see if anything helps Prim and Mason!"

"Agreed," all three witches replied in unison. The girls joined hands so that Blue could show them the details of her early morning premonition.

Bluebell closed her eyes, and they zipped their lips. A daffodil shaped clock from the '60s ticked loudly in the hallway. Blue centered herself around the sound, focusing on memories. Her lids snapped open a few seconds later, exposing the whites of her eyes. A scene appeared, hovering just above the wooden table.

The projection presented them with a faceless Bluebell in a loose white dress. She stood over a wide crack in the floor of a cave. Steam vented upward, wrapping warm tendrils around her body. One of Blue's hands twitched, and sweat broke out on her forehead from the warmth of the memory.

"Wait!" Iris was always good for an interruption. "Were you pregnant here?"

"Of course, she was pregnant," Clover said and rolled her eyes.

"No, *seriously*," Iris pressed the issue. "Were you pregnant in the dream, Blue? Did you feel pregnant? Or see your face in a mirror?"

"It's a cave; who puts mirrors in caves?" Hyacinth asked. "And she's not far enough along to tell by her face —that's just mean, by the way. Let her get on with the vision."

"It's always got to be about Iris somehow." Clover debated removing her hands to choke the cheery plastic bear in effigy.

"I don't know." Bluebell paused, her eyes rolling forward. "I don't recall seeing my face, so maybe not."

"Aha!" Iris said and turned, glaring at Clover for several seconds before holding her hand out and flicking it from the wrist several times in a swift, magnanimous gesture. "Sorry for the distraction. Go ahead, Blue."

Bluebell closed her eyes, starting the process all over again. The steam shifted in front of them, forming rough shapes. There was a distorted voice; it was too deep and garbled to make out any of the words.

"Your sound quality is shit." Iris naturally assumed that commentary from a music lover on the matter was helpful. "You need some kind of vision equalizer to adjust the frequencies."

Hyacinth sighed. "Seriously, stop it! It's her vision. Just hush and let her show us the story the best way she can. Please?"

Bluebell's eyes opened first, then her mouth. She shut it and yanked her hand away, drumming her fingers on the table for several seconds. She stared pointedly at the remaining muffins.

Why did she subject herself to this gaggle of attention-deficient ingrates? They didn't even realize she had better things to do with her time than bake for them. With a look that loosely translated to "thank the Goddess I'm only having one of you," she shook her head and closed her eyes again.

It took a bit longer to get back into the vision this time. The steam eventually appeared and assumed the shape of a horned lion, symbolic of the demon Ipos. It faded out, replaced by a whirlwind of items: the locket, a timepiece, and a wedding ring with a ribbon tied around it.

The objects tumbled, around and around each other, in the air. The garbled voice (whose quality *had* improved a bit) said something about lesbians, or Succubae, or both, and an army, and somebody's dead body. It didn't make much sense, but that was still how it went.

The lion and the juggling act faded away, replaced by a smaller animal, something like a rat or a cat. A dog materialized beside it, growing until it appeared to be more of a wolf (Mason?). The wolf growled and snarled, circling the rat-cat; somehow, that felt wrong, like it shouldn't have been happening, yet was necessary, to all of the girls.

"Maybe the rat-cat was a ferret; they're..." Clover and Hyacinth glared at Iris together this time. Iris scrunched up her nose and glared back. She pantomimed locking her lips and throwing away the key—with a grand finale of shooting a flaming bird with a proud middle finger at Clover. "Go on with your dream-story."

A flower formed from the midst of the battle, the two creatures dissolving into it. The steam took the shape of five rounded blobs around the blossom, and the blobs became the fingers and thumb of a hand. The hand methodically plucked away at the petals until there was only one left.

"That's it." Bluebell opened her eyes as the image faded. "I woke up with Prim's name on my lips. Also, I thought I smelled bacon, which is weird because I don't even like meat."

"Ahem." Iris pretended to clear her throat, making a hundred percent sure that Bluebell was done this time before she said anything.

"Yes?" Bluebell was afraid to ask, and, yet, she did. "I think I can explain the bacon."

Clover cracked her neck and muttered, "Unbelievable."

"Not the most important part," Bluebell said, "but, okay, now I'm curious. Go ahead."

"It was her vision, not yours," Iris replied.

"Whose?" Clover and Hyacinth asked the question together.

"Baby Huxley!" she answered triumphantly. "That's why you didn't feel pregnant and why you smelled bacon. She was trying to tell you she's not a vegetarian."

"You are chock full of shit!" Clover shouted. "So a demi-god knocked up Blue. Fine, but that's still just a baby she's carrying, it's not the stinking Oracle of Delphi bopping around in there."

"Huh," Bluebell said as the kitchen table vibrated angrily in response. "I'm guessing none of you girls did that?"

"Nope." Iris was more than happy to gloat. "And don't you worry, sweet little oracle. Auntie Iris might not approve of your food choices, but she's better than your Auntie Clover, and she'll always have your back."

"Don't listen to Auntie Iris about your Auntie Clover," Clover spoke up to ensure she was heard, "your Auntie Iris is a narcissistic asshole!"

"Language!" Hyacinth hissed, looking over at Bluebell. "And I drove them here—I'm so sorry about this."

"It's fine," Bluebell laughed.

"No," Hyacinth insisted, reaching over to place a hand on her sister's belly, "it isn't. Baby Huxley? It's your Auntie Hyacinth speaking. Please don't listen to all the bad words Auntie Clover and Auntie Iris use. Bad words are for grown-ups. You're not allowed to use them until you're, um, twenty-one."

"Shut the fuck up!" Iris burst into peals of laughter at the horrified look on Hyacinth's face. "Seriously, what are you thinking? That's the legal drinking age, Cyn. We're witches, not nuns."

"Yeah," Clover giggled, finally getting into the spirit. "Don't worry, your Auntie Iris, and Auntie Clover will have you tattooed and swearing like a dockworker long before then."

Chapter 6
THE MAGIC

Never in her life had Primrose regretted anything more than the walls she had knocked down to create an upstairs loft.

"Powers of the East, Guardians of the Air,

I consecrate this mirror.

I charge it with your energies.

Purify this tool and render it sacred."

There was too much intimacy, and no doors to hide behind, with him in her sanctuary.

"Powers of the South, Guardians of the Fire,

I consecrate this mirror.

I charge it with your energies.

Purify this tool and render it sacred."

Even on the opposite side of an expansive room, she felt Mason's eyes on her body, the same way she once had his hands.

"Powers of the West, Guardians of the Water,

I consecrate this mirror.

I charge it with your energies.

Purify this tool and render it sacred."

Primrose cleared herself of any residual negative energy, named what she had consecrated as her own, and returned to Mason's side. She knelt on shaky legs beside the coffee table and set the bowl with the black salt down, placing the small table mirror inside of it.

"What's the mirror for?"

"The same purpose as any other mirror." She took off her glasses and placed them on the table between them. "*Reflection.* This mirror will catch the magical energy reflected into it from an item—trickery, love spells, a little bad juju—and bounce it back to its sender."

"There's something wrong with your eyes, Rose." The vibrant red circles alarmed him. "Does this have something to do with the spell?"

"I've consecrated the objects, but there's no other magic at work yet. What you're looking at is a permanent gift from Hell," she answered as if they were talking about the weather. Why not let him see a hint of what was wrong with her? Maybe it would scare him away for good. "You might call it the demonic version of LASIK."

"How did it happen?"

"I spent some time in the realm," she said, "thanks to an inescapable obligation; you're looking at one of the side effects."

"Tell me what happened and why you were there."

"I prefer not to talk about it." There was no point in explaining that it was his fault, not after all these centuries.

"And the glasses?"

"Most of what I glimpse is demonic; ugly stuff, not something you'd want to deal with 24/7. The lenses were crafted to stifle it." She held out a hand, wiggling her fingers for the ribbon. "But I need to see the nature of the bridal beast now to confirm my suspicions."

"About Brunhilde." Mason held out the token grimly and watched Primrose snatch it away from him.

"If your wife is what I think she is, the Germanic name's a lie—that's probably not even her nickname. Demons never divulge their true titles. Honestly, hers is most likely twelve syllables long and more easily spoken in some ancient tongue like Aramaic."

"Brunhilde was never my mate, Rose."

"And *now* you know what an idiot you were," Primrose said and busied herself, nestling the bright orange ribbon in a patch of salt adjacent to the mirror's glass. "You're welcome."

"All in all, you should still consider yourself lucky," she continued, tilting the glass down a bit to capture the cloth's reflection. "Now, you can go back, hit the dating scene, and start looking for her. If I were you, I'd put up a billboard near one of those businesses of yours. The little bitches will be lining up around the block in no time."

"Little bitches?" he raised an eyebrow but looked pleased with her tone.

"Yes." She bit the inside of one cheek, tasting blood. Don't go there, Prim. Jealousy was a weakness, and weaknesses came with too high a price. "Correct me if I'm wrong, but I believe bitch is the appropriate term for wolves of the female persuasion."

"The billboard won't be necessary. I found my mate a long time ago, and we both know she's not a shifter," Mason was determined as a hound dog digging up a buried bone.

"What I know is that you are inordinately cocky. Don't forget how wrong those bulletproof mating instincts of yours got it the first time around." Primrose flexed a crackling palm in the air to remind him of her power. She was no one's old bone, and far too dangerous to gnaw on these days. "I strongly suggest you allow me to clean up mess number one before you attempt to take this misguided conversation any further, Wolf."

"Sure thing, Sugar Britches," Mason said and winked at her.

There it was; the same old charisma the bastard had used to seduce her in the first place. Primrose desperately wanted to pick up the cheery orange fabric, light it on fire, and throw it into that handsome face. She closed her eyes instead, reconnected with her breath—in and out, out and in—and turned her mind to the matter at hand. No good ever came from a powerful witch working angry magic.

She held her hands out with her palms open over the mirror and the bowl. The energy from the orange cloth tickled her as she opened herself to it. Warmth flooded her belly, dipping lower; her body immediately responded to the invasion.

Prim took a deep shuddering breath, allowing sensations she'd abstained from for hundreds of years to wash over her. Just as she'd suspected, Brunhilde was a sex demon, probably a Succubus. She sensed Mason staring and opened her eyes to glare. Considering what had just happened to her, it felt like an invasion of privacy.

"Don't look at me like that!" she snapped. "Look at the mirror, and watch the damned spell go to work."

"Your wish is my command, oh sexy one."

"*Redeat donum. Vultim revelaret.*" Primrose gritted the chant through her teeth. They both knew the wish he was talking about had nothing to do with her spell. The glass in the mirror turned elastic, shifting and spreading, before snapping back to a solid state again. Return the gift. Reveal the face. "Redeat donum. Vultim revelaret."

A thin stream of orange arose from the ribbon. It flowed toward the mirror and into it as the two of them watched. An image appeared on the other side—a voluptuous, red-skinned female with black hair and dark eyes.

Mason's counterfeit wife stood in the dressing room of a store, trying on couture club wear. The dizzying kaleidoscope of images Prim saw lingering around the Succubus—in this case, a mostly transparent shoplifter egged on by something gelatinous and greedy with a dark aura—confirmed the locale. She could never figure out whether the overlapping scenes she saw without her glasses were of the past, present, or future. The only purpose they seemed to serve was making her nauseous.

As for the Succubus, wanton energy rolled off her in waves. Prim was surprised to see that *her* aura was an expected honeycomb of both light and darkness. Her red shoulders shivered as the energy from the token returned to her. She looked deep into the mirror with a lick of her lips and a smile, addressing Primrose.

"Hello to you, too, bright eyes—that's a hell of a way to introduce yourself."

"Your hold on Mason is gone." Primrose didn't waste any time; she wanted those glasses back on as soon as possible.

"Then I owe you a favor; no offense, but I never wanted him. Be sure and give that wolf of yours a great big kiss to celebrate. Use a little tongue; see what happens. Oh, and, between you and me, you might want to clean up the place afterward. There's bound to be an unwelcoming party coming at some point, headed by your determined groom to be."

"Can you tell me how to stop him?" a somewhat startled Primrose rushed to ask the question for fear the image would begin to fade.

"Honey," the demon laughed, "I'm his cousin, not a miracle worker. If I knew that, Ipos would have been dead long before now."

"What about the locket?" Mason leaned forward so the Succubus could see his face. "It belongs to Rose's family."

"Sorry. It's no longer in my possession."

"Alright, Brunhilde," Mason answered. "Is there anything you can tell us that might be helpful?"

"The name's Borana," she said. "And, Primrose, you should talk to your sisters. Love is a powerful bond; Ipos has made you fear it because he does. That doesn't mean you should—anything he fears might be a valuable weapon."

Mason sat in silence, watching her after the conversation ended. Primrose returned the glasses to the bridge of her nose without comment and cleansed the residual energy from the items. Afterward, she locked them away in an oak banded trunk, on the opposite side of the loft, beside her bed.

Borana's talk of kissing had been unfortunate and cruel; with Mason, even something as simple as a kiss could be dangerous. Primrose had no idea how the dark part of her would respond if she allowed Mason to rekindle all the old feelings that came with their past. If it didn't kill him, a real mating bond might very well infect him.

On the bright side, the vibe they picked up from Borana was surprising. The Succubus's aura was so mixed it was almost neutral, and, if her comments about Mason were genuine, then Ipos had dealt Borana a cruel hand, as well.

Primrose shook off her thoughts long enough to head back to the kitchen, placing the bowl of meat for her friend in the alley inside the refrigerator.

"You're free of her now," she told Mason. "I trust you to honor your word about remaining silent for Hyacinth's sake."

"Of course," he followed her to the door.

"Good," she nodded, sliding on her shoes and gesturing at Mason's to indicate he do the same. "Then our business is concluded. She no longer has the locket; I can go back to work, and you can go home."

"Now, that's where you're wrong," he said, slipping his feet back into his cap-toed leather oxfords. "Our business is just beginning, Rose. You're in danger, and I'm not going anywhere."

"This isn't up for argument, Mason."

"I agree with you; it isn't."

Her shoulders tensed as she offered the obligatory threat, "One way or another, I can make you go. If I do, I promise, it will not be pleasant for you."

"I'm not afraid of you," he said.

"You should be. I'm not joking when I say that I can hurt you in ways you can't even imagine, Mason."

"I know," Mason didn't doubt she could hurt him, just not in the way she was thinking, "but I'm still not going anywhere. You need me here; you're in danger."

"That's nothing new," she said, her voice tinged with bitterness. "It's been that way since the day I was born."

"Something I made worse by abandoning you in Anjou. I'm not doing that again, sweetheart. I'm using your phone to make a call and have some of my things dropped off at the boundary. Clear it with whoever you need to—it's not up for argument."

"I don't want you moving in with me," Primrose hissed as she opened the door, "or calling me sweetheart. I'm not that girl anymore. For Goddess's sake, we'll be the talk of the entire neighborhood."

"If they're anything like your eye doctor," he answered, following her down the stairs, "they'll all be delighted. Just as my little flower would have been."

"There are no petals left for you to pluck here, Mason; the part of me you knew died a long time ago." Primrose waved her hand and said the magic words. The wall shimmered and disappeared, and Volumes &

Vagaries welcomed them into its midst again. "Take my advice and run from this place, as fast as you can."

"I would, if I thought, for one minute, that what you say is true," he murmured, turning to trap her against the wall as it reappeared. "Let's take a little bad demonic advice and test this theory of yours instead, shall we?"

Primrose stiffened her lips and closed her eyes. If he wanted to kiss her, fine, she'd just think about something else until the stubborn wolf finished.

She started at the beginning of the Dewey Decimal System, 000 Generalities—next came 010 Bibliography, and then 020 Library and Information Sciences, and 030 was General Encyclopedic Works. Dear *Goddess*, his breath was warm. Had it always been that warm?

Never mind, back to the System: 040 Unassigned. He was taking his sweet time, the bastard. 050 General Serials and their Indexes. 060 was Soft Lips sliding over her own, and a Slick Tongue probing and entering. No, that wasn't 060—why was she moaning? Damn it, how could she have forgotten about 060, and why did the man's mouth have to feel so right?

Primrose gave in to him, tentatively, at first. Tendrils of the power that sadist had awakened in her responded, too. It ebbed and flowed in contentment for the moment, not particularly bent on the destruction of anything. The only incident was an accidental spark that leaped from her tongue to his.

She opened her eyes to find Mason staring back at her, his eyes a deep, glowing gold.

"See?" His voice came out all growly, his mouth breaking into a smile before he let her go. "That wasn't so bad, now, was it?"

"It was a kiss; that's *all*." She shoved him away, embarrassed for the first time in ages. Moaning? *Really?* There would be no protection from the man's incalculable arrogance after this. "Don't go getting any stupid ideas about it meaning anything more than it should. You'll still be sleeping on the couch or the floor for as long as you insist on being here."

"As I believe I have proven," he said before walking away with a cockiness she remembered all too well, "the girl I once knew is still alive and kicking in there. That means all things between us are now open to negotiation, my wicked little Rose."

Chapter 7
THE DEAL

"Prisma Huxley, it has been far too long," the man said as he leaned forward. He placed his cheek against the dark-haired witch's—left, then right—and made obligatory kissing noises. "And you're looking even younger than the last time we met. How do you do it? "

"Cut the crap, psychopath." Primrose's grandmother eyeballed the figure that sat across from her in the outdoor tea garden. She abandoned her half- eaten raspberry scone for a freshly poured cup of Earl Gray with two and a half lumps of sugar. "We both know I am incapable of aging *or* getting younger, so the flattery is useless. What brings you here?"

"Really?" Ipos crossed his arms over the chest of the good-looking Frenchman he had worn for the occasion. "*Mon vieil ami, vous me blessez profondément*—you wound me deeply, old friend."

"Demons can't afford feelings or visit friends they don't have. And speaking French and explaining what you've said makes you sound like a pompous ass. Now *what*, precisely, do you want from me?"

"You've always been so mean to me," he pouted, looking around them. Disgustingly cheery butterflies darted through patches of raspberries, mint, and Angelica. "Ever thought about investing in some wolfsbane and hemlock, maybe a little nightshade, to liven this place up?"

"This place is a bed and breakfast," Prisma responded, taking a final bite from the flaky scone before dabbing at the corners of her mouth with a napkin, "not a murder in progress."

"Yes, but I haven't lost faith in you. You were so delectably evil back in the days when you were worth wooing. Surely you see the benefits in sprucing up this bastion of boredom."

"I'll do so when pigs fly," the witch answered. "I retired from that particular game, and I have been for a while now."

"I'm tempted to find a pig and a catapult just for you, but we'll have to save the antics for another day. That's not why I came."

"Do tell."

"You still work a spell here and there, from time to time, to keep the skills sharp. Don't you, *ma chère sorcière*?" He locked eyes with her across the table.

"That depends on who wants to know," she tilted her prized, peony-patterned teakettle and streamed tea into a saucer for Ipos.

Rich bergamot filled the air. The demon glared but took a large sip of the fragrant liquid at her insistence. "It saddens me to see you here, surrounded by a steady flow of strangers, still so lonely and unlucky in love."

"You don't give a damn about anyone other than yourself, and I am a Huxley, after all," she responded with a shrug. "The die was cast a long time ago."

"But we all deserve love, don't we?" Ipos leaned back in his chair, eyeing her intently. "You, your granddaughters ... me."

"*You?* Deserving of love?" Prisma nearly snorted tea out of her nose, "And you say it so sincerely! That's a tall order, asking anyone to love a fiend like you."

"Oh, you misunderstand me." His voice deepened as he leaned forward in the lavender cushions of the dainty white chair. The fires of Hell reflected for a moment in his eyes. "I won't be asking for it; I will be commanding it."

"Okay. I think I've heard just about enough out of you." She stood abruptly, tossing her napkin on the table between them. "Those girls already despise me, and there's a good reason; I drove their mother insane and ruined one of their lives. There's nothing you could offer me that would convince me to help you trap Primrose into spending the rest of her immortal life in your company."

"Oh, believe me, I understand," Ipos replied with a cunning smile, "and, yet, I am here to change your mind."

"How?" Prisma challenged the beast.

"Quite easily. I just so happen to have, in my possession, the one thing you've been looking for, for centuries."

"You're going to have to be more specific than that."

"It's a piece of jewelry that makes a human immortal, as you designed it to do, thus extending the curse to a companion of your choosing," Ipos said. "You lost track of it a while ago, and it ended up in the hands of a wolf. Does that ring any bells with you?"

"With a wooden mallet, yes," Prisma replied.

"Funny thing; no one downstairs has been able to figure out who you made that bargain with to get it."

"I'm not surprised," that was all she was going to say on the matter. "Why are you suddenly feeling so generous?"

"Because I don't need it anymore. The thing I now desire, more than anything else in all of the worlds, my dear Prisma, is to have your granddaughter, Primrose, back in my arms again. And the question you should be asking yourself is not why, but how badly do you want that trinket back."

"Forever the Faustian drama queen, aren't you?"

"I prefer 'skilled thespian'—and that's ironic, you know. Considering the original Faust was damned for preferring human knowledge over the divine—a pointless endeavor, as far as I'm concerned."

"Divine infers a god or a goddess is at work. You qualify as neither of those things and, believe me, none of them want anything to do with you, Ipos."

"The gods are dead."

"Not dead—faded."

"They're spirits, fine; let's not get bogged down in semantics," Ipos answered. "Besides, nowadays, 'divine' can denote anything from deific to spectacular. I *am* truly spectacular, by the way, and I didn't come here to argue the finer points of theology with a pagan. Are you interested in making a deal with me or not?"

"Possibly," Prisma looked around the empty garden for a moment, rubbing the back of her neck. She picked up a small hand bell to signal the wait staff for a cleanup before inviting him to follow her and discuss things further. "Anything is preferable to your subjecting me to the long list of accolades you force your servants to recite daily."

"Now, *this* is how I pictured you living," Ipos said, slipping into the private study to which Prisma had led him. "Dark items surrounding you and not a single piece of vomitous shabby chic in sight."

The thickly patterned carpet vibrated with residual djinn's magic. An eclectic assortment of swords, dolls, and masks decorated the walls around him. Two of the sabers caught Ipos's attention; he was certain they had belonged to Napoleon's Imperial Guard.

Prisma gestured to a seat across from her on a beige and brown striped sofa. Tassels decorated it, along with wooden elk legs and a faded bloodstain smack-dab in the middle. It had strands of black and white from a cat that was suspiciously absent. Ipos brushed them away before sitting.

"I'm running a successful business. It's all about the image," she answered. "People want to feel cozy and loved; they want a story. Load a bed and breakfast with estate sale items, convince them you've inherited your dear, sweet grandmother's property in the country, and they'll pay extortionist fees just to get a room."

"If only they knew what you were."

"They wouldn't believe it," Prisma smoothed a wrinkle from her vintage tea gown, one of several period pieces she occasionally wore for the effect. "Now, tell me what you want with Primrose. I thought you'd have a family of your own by now."

"I have no family, only relatives, and associates," the demon replied, "and none of them are compliant or suitable."

"Suitable?"

"For marriage—unlike Primrose, who suits me to a T after our time together and your delightfully nefarious bargain."

"Your *time together*? So you're trying to spin it as collaboration now?" Prisma chuckled. "Don't lie to me, Old Boy. I hear your *time together* was somewhat one-sided and incredibly violent."

"I didn't realize you still talked with the girls, considering how despicable they find you."

"I don't, but news travels fast in magical communities. I still have quite a few contacts alive and doing surprisingly well out there, from Morocco to New Zealand."

Ipos scraped well-manicured fingernails over the bloodstain on the fabric. Was this the spot where she had killed her own daughter's true love? "You, of all people, should know how hard it is to reach something that deeply hidden inside of a soul. Unleashing it required scurrilous actions."

"I do. As a matter of fact, I even felt your blade. She's a part of my bloodline, after all; I believe all the Huxley women experienced you and your perverted carving skills, to some extent, in our nightmares. Thankfully, most have forgotten it."

"You flatter me."

"Witches never take a violation of that degree lightly, Ipos. Many would just as soon see you eviscerated slowly for it."

"What about you?" Ipos asked.

Prisma paused. "There was a hard bargain struck for that locket, and, as we both know, a price paid cannot be undone. It would be a shame for me to have gained nothing for all my efforts."

"You are a wise woman," the demon responded with a nod, "one who deserves companionship. For what it's worth, I don't intend to hurt Primrose any more than necessary. I can assure you, the worst of the torture is behind us."

"You just want to expand her horizons now, and help her become all that she can be?"

"Exactly."

"I suppose that's not unreasonable," Prisma said. "It's almost noble, considering that it's you. But why a love spell?"

"Because Primrose loves someone else, a wolf shifter. Unfortunately, she recently discovered that the mutt in question loves her in *return*. I tried other means before coming. There was a Succubus from my family tree, Borana, but she lacked the proper ... commitment to succeed."

"Well, I certainly know how much you hate *wolves*," Prisma offered her hand to the demon to seal the deal, "and they say true love will never bring anything but heartache for Huxley women. It's that dreaded curse."

"So true," Ipos agreed.

"The *illusion* of love, now—that's nothing like the real thing. I foresee this deception being beneficial for the both of us. Especially if Primrose truly is as powerful as you think."

"You know," Ipos leaned back, crossing the legs on his cultured body. He watched Prisma opening boxes and drawers. She hummed loudly—something that sounded like Chopin—as she moved about, compiling the necessary items to change someone's heart. "It's a shame the rest of the witches in your family aren't more like you; they could learn a great deal."

"Oh, *darling*, you have no idea," Prisma walked back to him with a shiny pair of scissors in hand. "I've obtained locks of hair from practically everyone in the family tree over the years for, well, let's just call it insurance. So, all I need now is a lock of yours to get started on that love spell."

"I'd have to alter this form." Ipos balked at the idea of losing any fraction of his mane, however small. "And you don't even have the locket yet—it's not on me."

"Vanity *now*, dear? Do you realize how trivial that is when you're so close to success?" Prisma waved the sharpened object in the air and stared back at him, shaking her head. "Consider it an act of faith on my part. I have no doubt you will give the locket back to me, and I'll pick a spot that's barely noticeable."

Chapter 8
THE REJECTION

"You shouldn't be going out." Iris's voice sounded miffed on the phone. "Things are about to get serious for Prim. I'm not kidding; some crazy stuff could go down any minute now."

"Are you shitting me?" Clover responded as the cab driver pulled up in front of Kingdom Come. "*This* is how you think my life works? Everybody else but me gets to have fun? I need a night out, and I need it badly, Iris. You cannot guilt me into inviting you. We both know you don't want to see me working my mojo in the club."

"Gross."

Clover's tone turned defensive as she asked, "Homophobic much?"

"No," Iris huffed back at her. "I'm *Clover*-phobic. Don't be such a judgy bitch. The only reason it's creepy at all is that it's you."

"Alright, you get a pass, but don't call me judgy again. Stop whining and say goodnight, Iris. Remember to tell your platonic roommate hi for me the next time you wipe all the drool marks off him."

"I hate you."

"Same to *you*, sweetie. My cell phone is silent, starting now. Don't call unless there's an emergency."

Clover shut off her phone and pulled the wallet from her back pocket to pay the Yeti shifter behind the wheel. His driving skills were decent, but he kept the AC in the car 10-15 degrees too cold and disregarded all complaints. The modest gratuity she handed him before stepping out onto the sidewalk told him so.

In spite of its creepy asylum façade and the rather intimidating name, Kingdom Come maintained neutrality on almost every front. There were only two rules that its proprietor, a gargoyle named Mac, enforced on the premises. Never reveal your powers to those without magic, and never, ever fight epic battles for good and evil.

Clover ran a hand through her lightly spiked green hair, considering the reflection that greeted her in a patch of faded glass. A flick of her hand summoned a gust of wind to buff the surface, and she checked her makeup. Pale gloss coated plump lips. Vivid blue and green shadow highlighted her almond-shaped brown eyes to perfection. Beneath all of that, the tough-girl glamor lived up to its promises with a cowl neck top, tight jeans, and boots spiked enough to secure railroad ties.

"Hey there, hottie," she winked at herself before walking into the lobby.

"Good evening," the cracked statue in the dried up fountain greeted her. "Name and designation, please?"

"Clover Huxley. Witch."

"Thank you, Ms. Huxley. How will you be paying for entrance this evening?"

"*Libenter hoc magica tactu*—I freely give this touch of magic," she placed her hands on the statue in reply.

The residual breeze kicked up a few leaves around the granite figure. Within seconds, the door beyond the statue opened to the thump of bass. Neon lights bathed an entire sea of sweat-slick, half-naked bodies dancing and writhing inside the building.

"It's been a while," she thrust her shoulders back and put some swing in her hips, making her way to a corner seat at the bar, "but Mama is most definitely home."

The bartender scuttled over with a whiskey—neat, the way she liked it—in its hands. "I'm surprised to see you here tonight."

"Don't remind me," she groaned, "I've stayed away much longer than intended. Looks like business is still crazy good for you, though. Old Stony must be turning one hell of a profit with all this magic, huh?"

"Yeah." the creature shuffled from its first foot onto the second, then onto a third. "But that's not what I meant. There's a lot of talk going around about your family. Trouble brewing with a demon, or something to that effect."

"It figures," she sighed, downing the drink in one slug and handing the empty glass back to him. After sparing a glance at several of the lovely, sweaty figures gyrating on the dance floor, she accepted the second dose. "My family has to ruin everything, even the chances of my getting laid tonight."

"Be grateful they're not trying to tell you who to sleep with," a husky voice said. The incredibly warm body that went with it took up residence on the bar stool beside her.

Clover shifted in her seat and turned her head. She discovered one voluptuous, red-skinned honey of a demon on her left. Sexual energy oozed from the creature; it wasn't just Clover responding to it, either. Everyone in the vicinity seemed to be sweating or blatantly staring.

"Let me guess." Clover glanced down through the laces on the front of a spectacular corset dress—she couldn't help herself—before signaling the bartender. "Succubus, right?"

"Yes," the demon sounded amused, "but I do have a name aside from that, you know. It's Borana. Are you going to tell me yours, lean and green, or am I supposed to guess?"

"Clover," she offered, with a wry smile at the flicker of recognition. Lesson number one: As a Huxley girl, the reputation of the curse *always* precedes you. Despite being shit out of luck—that whole Succubus and men thing—Clover decided there was no harm in flirtation. "Let me buy your next drink, oh buxom Borana. Or do I have to get down on my knees and beg for the privilege?"

Borana raised an eyebrow at the woman. Was that confidence, a sense of humor, or both? Regardless, there was nothing to buy; the magical price of admission covered everything in Kingdom Come. She looked Clover up and down as if the idea of some knee-time had serious merit for the both of them before allowing her new favorite witch to signal the bartender.

Borana looked into Clover's big, brown eyes when the creature came over. She winked and announced with a wicked smile, "I'll have a

Screaming Orgasm."

The Puma shifter opposite Borana fell off the bar stool, flat on his back, like an idiot. Several curious patrons with enough sense to see the Humpty Dumpty act coming jumped back to avoid him.

"So much for a cat always ending up on its feet, huh?" Clover watched Borana's eyes light up with laughter as the shifter stumbled off.

"Yes, well," Borana took a generous sip from an ice-free glass, layered with vodka, amaretto, and cream liqueur, "males, in general, are still quite primitive, aren't they? All that chest beating, stomping and posturing to make them feel like they're the ones in charge. It's sad."

"You'll get no arguments from me," Clover answered thoughtfully. She took another drink and set her glass down, rubbing her palms on the tops of her thighs. What in the hell was with the sudden nerves?

"Listen, Borana—I know this may sound forward of me or, hell, maybe old-fashioned. Either way, feel free to say no, but I'd be kicking myself forever after if I didn't ask: Would you like to dance?"

The demon leaned in and crooked her finger, beckoning Clover to come closer to hear the answer. She placed soft lips next to the shell of Clover's ear. Her long, agile tongue snaked out to lick at the sensitive skin.

"Clover Huxley, there is nothing in this world, or any other, that I would rather do than dance with you. But I can't, and you need to go home. Your family has enough problems with Hell right now; you and I getting together would only complicate things further."

Borana moved, and Clover grabbed her forearm without even thinking. There was no way she was letting the owner of that tongue just slip from the bar stool and disappear into the crowd. "And once the problems are *solved*, what about then?"

"If you still want me," Borana said, her smile tinged with sadness as she removed Clover's hand, "after everything you have learned, then, *yes*, I promise. I will find you, and you and I will have that dance."

Clover turned back around as the only female she wanted for the evening, possibly the rest of her life, departed. She stared at the half-empty Screaming Orgasm and thought back on their conversation. Had the Succubus been teasing?

An Incubus with incredibly bad timing picked that moment to plop his tight panted butt down in the seat beside her. The bastard had sleazy sideburns, a goatee, and reeked of expensive cologne. Worst of all, he was already shaking his head like he understood her plight.

"*Women*, huh?" He gave his sexiest smile and leaned closer. "Don't worry about it, I've got something that'll make it all bet..."

"Shut the fuck up!" Clover tossed the remainder of Borana's abandoned drink in his face. She pushed her way through a crowd of startled faces, toward the entrance of Kingdom Come.

Iris was right. Things were about to get serious and not just for Primrose. One way or another, Ipos—the demon that was now messing up Clover's sex life—was going *down*.

Chapter 9
THE CHALLENGE

"Excuse me, Mr. Géroux?" A sugary-sweet voice followed the ringing of the bell at the front counter. "Could you be a darling, please, and help me again? There's a big heavy book on the top shelf down aisle three that I need."

Primrose rolled her eyes at the braless yoga fairy. This trip made visit number three. Up until Mason had started helping out, the limber lady (and lady was a *loose* term) had refused to set one toe into Volumes & Vagaries.

Prim wasn't sure half the females now frequenting the place could even read. They certainly weren't running home to scour the random volumes on taxidermy, warfare, and agriculture that they won in the "Watch Mr. Sexy Pants Climb The Ladder For You" game.

"I'm not paying you for this," she muttered as he went out of his way to saunter down her aisle on his way to the counter.

Mason gripped her shoulders lightly, brushing the entire length of his body against her. He breathed in her ear, and she stiffened in response, "Jealous much, Rose?"

There was no doubt about it; the bastard was torturing her. Instead of feeling safe with him around, she felt thirty-three kinds of amped up and frustrated. He might be obeying her rules in the loft—sleeping on the couch, turning his back when asked, and *finally* keeping his nakedness behind the damned shower curtain—but downstairs in the store was a different story.

"This is not jealousy, this is *annoyance*," she hissed while he slipped away.

"Keep telling yourself that," he slung the words back over one shoulder.

Primrose growled in response, moving a hand from the books she'd been arranging on the shelf. She flicked her fingers in his direction as he approached the braless wonder and spat out, "*Quod severis metes!*"

As you sow so shall you reap—the words had been instinctual, an afterthought meant to give the wolf a dose of his own stupid medicine. Unfortunately, the spell came out with too much power behind it. The ladder down aisle three responded by flying straight for the hot little hussy with the perky boobs at the counter. Along the way, it burst into flames.

"No!" Primrose shrieked, horrified at what she'd done. Mason dove for the yoga slut to save her from becoming fried chicken. Prim ordered the fire to cease; the ladder hit the floor, with icicles glued to its rungs, on the opposite side of their bodies.

"Please forgive me; I am so sorry," she apologized as she came out from the aisle, cringing and wringing her hands. "Are you alright? Let me get you a..."

"I'm fine!" the wide-eyed fairy peeled Mason's hands off her arms as fast as she could. She scrambled backward and skirted around the ladder, toward the door, rambling the whole time. "Couldn't be better! Don't worry about the book, Mas—um, sir. I don't need it anymore, and I have to go. Bye!"

"Thanks a lot, Mason," Primrose stared blankly at the ladder. "This is *truly* a new low for me. I've never attempted to murder a customer before."

"I'm pretty sure you're good there, Rose," Mason dusted an ash or two off his shoulders. "She wasn't buying anything this time."

Primrose bypassed the endearment; she was getting used to hearing them. "What are you talking about—she asked you to get her a book, didn't she?"

"Flirty Gertie had no purse and no pockets," he responded with excessive eyebrow wiggling, "and it's not like she had a bra to hide her credit cards and cash. Face it, she just wanted to get me up the ladder so she could look at my sweet..."

"Damn it, Mason!" Primrose held up a hand to stop him. "No one cares about your package."

"Your Freudian slip is showing, dirty girl," he picked up the ladder-turned-icicle and headed for the dumpster in the back alley. "I was going to say *butt.*"

Primrose followed him out of the door, surprising him a bit as she looked around for the bowl of meat she'd placed outside earlier in the day.

"*What?*" she responded, "This is *my* place, remember? You're the one who's imposing, not me."

Why don't you just admit it?" He tossed his cargo in the massive green dumpster, and it landed with a crash. "You were following me to make sure no harm comes to this lady-magnet ass of mine in the alley."

"Why you *insist* on pushing buttons that might get you incinerated is beyond me," Primrose said. "And, no, for your information, I am not safeguarding your posterior or your delusions about its magnificence. I wanted to make sure you weren't scaring my friend away."

"What friend?" Mason looked around as if he expected someone to walk up from out of the shadows and offer an introduction.

"King," she replied as if the name explained everything.

Mason turned to her. He didn't just turn; he towered, cocking his head and blinking expectantly. His eyes glowed faintly. Primrose assumed it was because he was waiting for an explanation—something that might make him happier about some other man's name on her lips.

She debated over whether or not to respond. *Stupid wolf.* It was turning him into a caveman, frustrating and possessive, and far more concerned about jealously—hers *and* his—than the fact she might obliterate him.

A meow solved their problem.

"Hello there, King," Primrose said and sank to her knees, holding out her arms to a black tomcat. He was close to the size of a dog, with a big white circle on his chest. "I was worried Mason had scared you away."

Mason laughed, looking down at the animal with the brass tag on its collar. "This is King?"

The feline held Mason's gaze as it walked to Primrose. Eerie blue eyes regarded him with disdain and, for some reason, the word "mutt" popped into his head.

Prim bowed her head for King, smiling as his cold nose and long whiskers tickled her skin. A strand of black fur stuck to her cheek. The cat rewarded her with a deep, booming purr.

"Rose," Mason frowned. "That little guy is marking you with his scent."

"Yeah." She remained where she was. "He's been coming around for years. We always do this."

The cat gave Mason a smug sideways look and continued to rub its face all over Primrose. The volume of the purring grew louder until it threatened to rattle the back of the dumpster away from the wall.

"Rose," Mason's demanded, his voice growing deeper. "*Stop* it. Now!"

King sat on his haunches and growled, not afraid in the least. Rose reached out and scratched behind one of his ears with her fingernails.

"It's alright, King, I *promise*." Primrose glared up into Mason's bright eyes. "No need to worry over the big, silly wolf. He's no threat to you."

"*Meow*." The tomcat licked forgivingly at a delicate spot between Primrose's thumb and forefinger. At the last moment, he sank the tip of his teeth into the overly sensitized spot to admonish her for the crappy quality of the company she kept. King glared at Mason, a challenge evident in his sparkling eyes before he turned and sauntered away.

"Get inside." Mason wrinkled his nose, not taking his eyes off King until the cat turned a corner past the alley.

"What is wrong with you?" Primrose stood up. "Are you insane? That's a cat."

"He marked you."

"Oh, my Goddess!" She stomped her foot. "Will you just stop being so primitive?"

"You need to go *inside* and *check* for customers," he placed a firm hand between her shoulder blades and pushed her back through the door.

"There's nobody in there. Even if they are, it's fine; no one shoplifts in Paradox."

"That's not what I'm concerned about," Mason said as he locked the entrance to the back alley. "Get the front door, Rose."

Primrose did as he said. Hair had sprouted on the back of his hands, a sign he was barely in control of his wolf. She came back with a question in her eyes.

"Upstairs," he told her, then added a "please" in response to the look she gave him.

Primrose removed the wall and led the way to the loft. Her heart pounded. She had never seen him shift before. If his wolf tried to hurt her, could she stop herself from killing him?

The door to the loft banged open. Mason scooped her off her feet, heading straight for the claw-foot tub.

"*No.*" There was fear in her voice, but it wasn't from a fear of him, "Mason, listen to me, what are you doing?"

"Getting his smell off you."

"It's okay; King only touched my hands and face. I'll wash it off in the kitchen sink."

"*No.* He *bit* you."

"Fine, I'll take a bath—just put me down!"

"No," Mason growled at her. He set Primrose on her feet by the tub and blocked her from running—a chase would do nothing to calm his wolf. His hands tore the shower curtain free of the rods suspending it from the ceiling.

"Turn around," she demanded. Her whole body shook, her teeth chattering from sudden nerves as she kicked off her shoes. "I can do this without you."

"No," Mason repeated himself in that same deep voice. He yanked the zipper on the front of her jeans down and wrestled the material from her hips.

She helped push the denim the rest of the way off, her mind racing. There had to be a way to get through to him. He couldn't see her like this, not the way that she was now.

Mason reached around her as she lifted the edges of her tank top. He twisted the knobs in the tub and tested the water with his wrist.

"Go away!" she punched him in the chest as hard as she could.

"No." Mason didn't even flinch. He turned her around to unhook her bra, then he stopped.

He *stopped* because he saw her skin.

"*Please*, just go downstairs." Her voice was tired as she took off her spectacles. "I told you; I've got this."

Mason removed her bra, ignoring what she had said. Carefully, almost reverently, he stroked the puckered scars. They started between her shoulder blades and progressed to the small of her back.

These weren't just scars; they were *symbols*.

He recognized some of them: the staff with two serpents coiled around it, the 8-pointed wheel of chaos, and the ouroboros, indicator of infinity. Others were completely unfamiliar. They all had one trait in common: craftsmanship. Ipos's handiwork showed exacting attention to detail; the demon had taken his time, and it must have hurt like hell.

"Rose?" Mason grew still; his voice was quiet. "*This* is what you didn't want to talk about?"

Primrose shivered. She wrapped her arms around the front of her body, using her forearms to cover the tips of her breasts. The grip of her fingers on her ribs stretched the bizarre occult roadmap the demon had cut into her skin.

"Yes."

"I'm so sorry," Mason placed a kiss on the small of her back as he knelt down to remove her last barrier.

"You don't have to be; you didn't do this to me, Mason."

"I'm going to kill him."

"You can't," she looked him in the eyes as he tossed her panties on top of the pile of clothes. "He's too powerful."

"No," he was relieved to see trust in her eyes for the first time in centuries, "you're too powerful. That's why he wants you so badly."

"It doesn't matter. There's no way for me to control it."

"I think there is, once you understand how a mating bond works." Mason placed her gently in the warm water. He kept his voice low and soothing as he reached around her.

Mason ignored her lavender-chamomile soap. He picked up the patchouli bar she had given him, instead—the one with his scent all over it. He dipped it into the water. "I mark *you*; you mark *me*; what's mine is yours. Afterward, you'll have the added strength of my wolf to help handle what's in you, and we can take on whatever that bastard throws at us. Together."

"It's too dangerous."

"No, it isn't," he bent down to lick the edges of her mouth. The hand bathing her right leg dropped the bar of soap into the water and moved higher.

"Oh, Goddess!" Primrose gasped, gripping the edges of the tub. "What are you doing to me?"

"That's not the Goddess," he assured her with a chuckle, "although I'm sure she approves. That's all me, sweetheart. And we're just finding out how dangerous you are."

"You can't."

"Alright."

She felt him smile against her lips as he stopped what he'd been doing.

"Maybe just this once?" she sighed.

The dark energy inside of her coiled and squirmed while Mason explored her mouth with his tongue. Her pupils dilated, her eyes flooding with red. Mason paid no mind. His hand trailed a slow path down the opposite thigh, retrieved the soap, and started all over again.

"The shop is closed, my beautiful Rose," his voice rumbled next to her ear, "and you and I are going to take all the time we need to test the limits of that tightly held control of yours."

"Please," she groaned as the soap hit the bottom of the tub with a *thunk* again, "it's been so long. I don't..."

"Don't worry, love." Mason nibbled on her earlobe, pressing her back against the tub. "We'll both be fine."

Chapter 10
THE BIRDS

"Explain yourself!" the force of Ipos's palm nearly cracked the table in half.

"You should have followed up sooner," Borana wasn't bothered in the least by his phone bullying; she had expected it. "I can't help you track them now—they negated that little enchantment I gave Mason."

"What do you *mean*?" He was already furious from discovering the chunk that butcher, Prisma, had taken from the back of his mane.

"N.E.G.A.T.E.D. You know, rendered it null and void," she answered and stared at her fingernails. The manicure part of her mani-pedi was *far* more impressive than all of his bellyaching. The ripe little 3D gel hearts, pierced by clover-draped green arrows, were perfect—so lifelike they were practically beating.

"How?"

"Your witch is smart—she bounced my energy back, made that ribbon just a ribbon and probably destroyed it. I bet they've even sealed the deal under the sheets by now. If I were *you*, I'd give up. Mason has his hands on everything you carved her up to access. That makes those two unstoppable, doesn't it?"

"Well, isn't that wonderful," Ipos snarled. "When were you planning on telling me?"

"Whenever it was a good time. You've been in such a bad mood lately that your mere presence in a room sucks all the positive energy out of it. That's terrible for my internal alchemy."

"Your what?"

"My sexual kung fu."

"First, you swear off meat and now this New Age nonsense! That stupid nanny that your father hired dropped you on your head too many times as a baby."

"It's entirely possible," Borana answered. "She always had her eyes on my daddy, not me, and she was *extremely* jealous of Mother."

"She was more than happy to act as an accessory to *both* of their murders when the time came," the lion-headed monster reminded her coldly before moving on. "Now that you have failed me completely, just be grateful I have a backup plan. If not for that, you'd be paying dearly, no matter how many friends in low places you think you have left."

"What plan?" Borana sat up in her chair. It startled the female at her feet so badly that she almost ruined the toe she had been painting.

"Too late to try and get into my good graces now," Ipos said, crediting her curiosity to all the wrong reasons. "I've taken the issue topside. Trust me; I am working with an expert in the field. If *anyone* can help me hunt down a Huxley witch, it's her."

"Who?"

"No one you know."

"Give me a name; you might be surprised. I've known lots of women topside quite well, and quite often, over the centuries. Everyone from kindergarten teachers to senators and minister's wives."

"Stop fishing." He used his *I'm disgusted with you* voice. "My connections are no longer of importance. You have failed me for the *last* time and no longer play even a minuscule part of my plans, Borana."

"That was *your* deal to begin with," she said. It was time to hang up before he figured out she had a weakness for a Huxley. "It's not like I care about a bunch of stupid witches."

"You look worried. That was CYA: Covering your ass, right?" The deadpan salon worker, one Borana suspected might be a golem, looked up and addressed her in a voice less monotone than usual.

"Yep," she replied, admiring her toes. "You did a great job on the hearts by the way. They're first rate; I don't think I've ever seen better work. And that guy I was talking to is my cousin Ipos. He's a pompous asshole who killed my parents, took my money, and wants to control my life."

"It's the same old story," the bony female confirmed with a nod. "If I had a gold coin for every time I heard it, I'd be guarding a pot at the end of a rainbow by now. For what it's worth, I've heard of this guy, and everyone I know of that's met him thinks he's an idiot. What with the chauvinism and crappy Regency attire, they say it's like he's living in a bad historical romance novel."

"I know, right?" Borana responded with gusto. "It's not like I haven't been warning him for years—*Hel-lo!* The early 1800's called and they want their clothes and that attitude back."

"So, the situation is all *fercockt*. I assume that means you're pretty much on your own and need some help."

"Fer-*what?*"

"That's Yiddish for all screwed up—hang around, I'll teach you some more," the creature answered. "*Now*, can I assume that you're pretty much on your own and need some help? "

"Yeah," Borana sighed. "How did you...?"

"I wasn't kidding about the if I had a wish thing." The golem stood up and cracked her back— an awful sound, punctuated with an *oy*— before walking over to the register. "This may come as a surprise to you, but I have connections that might be able to help someone in your unique predicament. So, come on, just between us girls, what is it you're looking for?"

"Wait, what's in it for you?" The Succubus was smart enough to be skeptical of people who used the phrase *unique predicament* after talking about how familiar something was.

"I *would* say the milk of human kindness, but neither of us is human, so we both know that's *bupkes*—worthless—to us." The golem held out empty hands to illustrate her point. "What do I *want?* I want a nice tip and for you to refer me some business."

"Done; is that it?"

"Just remember your dear Auntie Golem. *And* consider contributing substantially to her retirement, should you ever defeat The

Lion Shlemiel with his lamentable craving for cravats. I'm talking kick his butt well enough to reclaim your fortune, here—the mountain, not the molehill."

"Do you give that retirement speech to everybody?" Borana handed the creature a credit card tied to the house's substantial assets. She was starting to warm to dear old Auntie Golem.

"Everybody, *every* time. Considering I'm still on my knees, looking at feet half the day, you can see just how far all the grand talk has gotten me." Auntie Golem swiped the card and nodded decisively as an approval of the ridiculous fee she had entered popped up on the screen. "Good! That's more than enough lip flapping about me. Tell me your problem, leaving out none of the details, and I'll let you know who's going to solve it."

Borana smiled, really smiled, for the first time since she had to leave Clover in Kingdom Come. She took a deep breath and answered with complete honesty—something told her Auntie Golem could take it.

"I'm a lesbian Succubus, who met Clover Huxley (cursed witch) in a bar. She's a *total* hottie whom I'm dying to show my Cambodian alphabet trick; 74 letters and I'm not even kidding."

"Uh-huh. Cunning linguist—I get it."

"Complication: My lion-headed asshole of a cousin threatened to disown me unless I commandeered her oldest sister's mate. So, I tricked Primrose's wolf into thinking that he loved me, made him steal the infamous Huxley locket from her, and played 'hide the unwanted sausage' with him for centuries before I even *met* Clover."

"Wow," Auntie Golem said, "*Bubula*, everybody's heard of the Huxley family, but..."

"Not done: This was all to maneuver Primrose into a position that forced her to bargain with Ipos. She had no choice left but to agree to his terms if she wanted release from the naughty nun captivity he'd orchestrated. What Primrose *didn't* know was that Ipos intended to do something worse: carve a zillion occult symbols into her body to release the power Grandma Huxley put inside of her."

"Listen," Auntie Golem tried again, "there's *no way* we can..."

"Hold on," Borana answered, "please. I'm almost through, I swear.

Not too long ago, I came clear with Primrose, formally released her boyfriend, and gave them my blessing. *Then*, I met Clover. Now I find out my cousin has some backup plan for getting big sister Huxley and all her power back. Only he won't tell me how, or even who his new go-to gal is, because I refused to go back to the whole sucky heterosexual Succubus-wolf detail to help him."

"As I was trying to say," Auntie Golem replied, holding her dry palms up in self-defense, "this is *meshuga*—completely crazy. There's no way I can handle all of it."

"I know. It's not about solving everything, Auntie. I've never admitted it all out loud before, and it seemed like you would be a good listener."

"You need a fairy godmother, or a decent therapist, not a golem, honey. Pick something for us to tackle. What's it going to be, your love life or saving the big sister?"

"Clover would never forgive me if I didn't save her sister. Honestly, I don't think I could forgive myself. Poor Primrose has already suffered enough for several lifetimes. Wardrobe and popular opinion aside, my cousin truly is a dangerous psychopath."

"So, just to be clear, we start by warning the family this asshole's got a backup plan? And then you engage in a race against some presumed time crunch to figure out what it is and how to save Primrose?" Auntie Golem asked.

"Yes," Borana nodded, "just like they do in the movies. That's the plan."

"Wise decision, that. Raising the stakes makes things pretty darned exciting. Nobody is drooling in the popcorn or checking their watches."

"Exactly." Borana nodded. "Maybe we'll even get to blow up something. You can never go wrong with an explosion."

"Don't go getting ahead of yourself with pyrotechnics just yet. Things still need to make sense. We'll start by getting the word out, see what happens, and take it from there," Auntie Golem answered.

"Alright, but I *really* wanted to blow up something."

"I know, Bubula."

"How about gratuitous sex? I have a genuine need for it; I'm a Succubus."

"If this were a movie, whose would it be?" Auntie Golem prompted. "Come on, be honest. Who is the main protagonist here? Who gets to have all the hot, earth-shattering sex in the movie?"

"Primrose."

"And there's your answer," Auntie Golem said. "Your time will come, but it isn't today, lust bucket. Put a lid on all the panty boiling and let's get back to the question of the day: Message delivery. I don't recommend using mirrors—too predictable. We need to be creative in case TLS becomes as paranoid as everybody already assumes he is."

"TLS?" she asked.

"The Lion Shlemiel."

An hour later, Borana and her new toe art—showcased in fabulous, open-toed heels—wandered down the block. She muttered the instructions given to her and pouted over the hot lesbian action ban.

Auntie Golem's go-to for covert communications was some creepy old wraith that collected the spirits of homing pigeons. More specifically, these were birds that had been used exclusively by the French during WW1.

In the end, the so-called creepy wraith turned out to be a ghostly compulsive hoarder in an abandoned strip mall on the east side of Hell. The old spirit was neurotic, sure, maybe even annoying, but by no means full on creepy.

Borana figured it had to be the ectoplasmic crap stains and incessant cooing from the war pigeon spirits that pushed Auntie Golem's opinion over into the creep zone. Or maybe it was the horrendously stereotypical little berets and cigarettes the wraith made all the gray-winged ghosties sport. Either way, they sent five of them out, one to each of the sisters.

The message each of the birds carried read: Ipos is up to no good – stop – Says he has a backup plan – stop – Mysterious woman topside helping locate Primrose – stop – Be suspicious of anything weird – stop – Wait, other than this message – stop – B.

The harder Borana tried to explain that a paper note carried by a dead messenger pigeon didn't need to follow telegraph rules, the more the crazed hoarder stubbornly argued that, yes, it did. So Borana finally let it go. And she prayed to whatever Goddess (if any) was still listening to a lesbian Succubus in Hell, that one, or more, of the five Huxley witches, got the ridiculous message and, more importantly, the point.

Chapter 11
THE POINT

Hyacinth inhaled deeply from her position on the pink mat. She flowed from Sun Salutation into the four-limbed burn of her favorite Chaturanga pose, then into Upward Facing Dog.

As her back curved, she arched her chin toward a bothersome crack in the condo's ceiling. Intensifying the stretch, she kicked the structural flaw from her mind and focused on the sensation in her abdominal muscles, instead.

She exhaled and pushed her weight backward, raising her pelvis into the traditional Downward Dog position. Hyacinth was just starting to forget about all her jiggly bits when her cell phone rang on the coffee table.

"Fudge!" She glanced over at the darned thing, her heart rate accelerating. More blood—a dizzying amount considering how little she'd eaten—rushed to her head.

Primrose had recommended vinyasa yoga. She claimed it helped her come to terms, at least partly, with her trauma. Partly sounded better to Hyacinth than "not at all" or "total sobbing mess." And it was Prim who had liberated her from Preston's perpetual abuse in the first place.

All the stretching and flowing might work if people stopped calling. It wasn't like she didn't want to regain her powers; it was just that Preston had beaten all the confidence out of her. Every blow had come with words like fat, ugly, stupid, and worthless. He had said those hurtful things, over and over, until she finally believed him.

Of course, it wasn't real people calling, just sisters. Huxleys were the only ones who had her number these days. Two of them, in particular, insisted on dialing at all hours of the day and night: Clover and Iris.

"Hello?" Hyacinth kept her voice cheerful, despite the yoga buzzkill.

"Hi, Cyn!" Iris's voice was three decibels shy of a shout.

"Sorry, Hyacinth," Clover said. "We hadn't heard from you today, so we figured we ought to call."

Hyacinth cleared her throat. She looked around the small condo; the rental property belonged to the owner of a yoga supply store down the street. The downtown neighborhood was a little questionable, but it *was* quiet, and Preston's old pack mates couldn't find her here.

"It hasn't been that long, you know."

"Sorry, Hyacinth." Bluebell added her voice to what was now obviously a Huxley conference call before it went much further. "We didn't mean to interrupt whatever you were doing."

"Yoga," Hyacinth was embarrassed to imagine what else her sisters had been thinking. She was alone, trying to reconnect with her body and restore her powers—and all three of them had such dirty minds. "It was *yoga*, Blue; I was trying out some of the stuff Prim taught me."

"Oh, Sweetie," Bluebell said as her mothering instinct kicked in, "we're sorry to interrupt your practice, but it's important."

"What's important?" Hyacinth sat down on the nearest chair, which happened to be a hot pink and black balance ball with locking caster wheels. Half the furniture in the place was from an '80's Retro yoga product line. "Have you figured out how to help Prim yet? Did something happen to her?"

"Not yet," Iris sounded worried.

"You haven't been outside today, have you?" Clover asked.

"Today?" Hyacinth almost laughed at the question. Being a part of the world outside wasn't on the agenda. She hadn't been outside for quite a few days now. Not since Clover and Iris invited her to meet for lunch, and they ended up at Blue's. "No, not really. Why?"

"Just do us a favor," Iris said. "Open the front door and have a look."

"There's not going to be a flaming bag of dog poop on the doorstep, is there?"

"No, just trust us." It was Clover again. "We're not shitting you, I promise. Blue's on the line."

That was all she needed to hear; it always had been. Blue was number two, the second oldest. Primrose and Blue had never been in on any of the pranks when they were kids. It was always just sisters number three and four—good old Clover and Iris. The girls who got along like cats and water yet coordinated better than a SWAT team when it came to tormenting anyone else.

"Alright, but this had better be good."

"It depends on how you define good," Bluebell remarked somewhat wryly as Hyacinth unlocked two deadbolts and the tertiary chain ("better safe than sorry" was her motto on the front door, "but it's a sign."

Hyacinth looked at—well, technically, *through*—the pigeon hovering outside her door. Ethereal as the winged rat was, there was still a very real note clutched in its little feet. She reached out her hand and, sure enough, it let go. The parchment fell into her palm, and the messenger disappeared in a puff of smoke.

"What the...?" She opened the rolled up note and started reading as she shut the door and relocked the bolts and chain. "Okay, *weird*. I just saw a bird ghost—and this thing reads like a Western Union Telegraph from the 1800's. Are we hunting down Doc Holliday or helping Primrose?"

"It's not a joke," Bluebell answered. "At least, Baby Huxley and I and aren't getting that vibe. It appears to be a legitimate warning about Ipos."

"I'm so scared for Prim," Hyacinth said as she sank onto the sofa. "She can't control it; you saw what happened that night, and the only thing she wanted to do was protect *me*. Gran and Ipos did this to her, and now Ipos is coming after her. What are we going to do?"

"It's okay, honey," Clover answered for all of them. "One way or another it *has* to be. We'll figure out a way to make this right."

"Yeah." The voice was Iris's this time. "No one fucks with a Huxley girl and gets away with it! We're stuck together like glue."

"And some of us are just as toxic," Bluebell added, making Hyacinth giggle.

"Iris farted, didn't she?"

"No!" Iris said.

"Yes!" Clover and Bluebell insisted.

"Well, your muffins have too much fiber in them," a red-faced Iris complained.

"So, what about this message?" Hyacinth was determined to move the conversation along. Iris had been a giant methane bomb since their childhood; there was no sense in dwelling on it. "Do we know where it came from?"

"No."

"It says "mysterious woman topside"—I'm assuming it's got to be Hell. Does anyone other than Prim know somebody else in the neighborhood? It looks like there's a small B at the bottom," Hyacinth added.

"Nope," Iris responded.

"Clover?" Hyacinth asked. "You're awfully quiet over there. What's going on?"

"If I tell you this story, you have to promise not to judge me."

"Oh, you slut!" Iris shrieked. "I knew it! You met somebody that night at Kingdom Come didn't?"

"You went out clubbing while Primrose is still in danger?" Bluebell was not happy.

"My vagina was getting cobwebs in it," Clover said dryly. "And you're the one that told us it would take time for you to figure something out. Don't judge me, Princess Preggo-Bell."

Hyacinth snorted and then clamped a hand over her mouth. It was a bad idea to encourage Clover or Iris—*ever*.

"You went there after I called and told you not to go!" Iris wasn't through shouting yet. "That's who this B is, right? One of your tra-la-la-lollops from Kingdom Come! Am I right, or am I *right* here?"

"Her name," Clover sighed, "is Borana. And she's not one of my trollops. She's a Succubus."

"Wait," Hyacinth stopped her. "A what?"

"Talk about unlucky in love," Bluebell sighed. "I'm afraid you've got us all beat on that one."

"Yeah," Clover answered. "You might say that."

"Alright, Clover. This story sounds like something we all need to hear in person," Hyacinth said as she noticed a beep on her end of the phone. "Hold on a minute, okay? I think I'm getting another call."

"That's weird."

"Bullshit, nobody else has your new number except for..."

"Shut up and let her get it!"

"Hello?" Hyacinth picked up the other line.

"Sorry to bug you, Cyn, but it's Prim. I just got a weird message in Paradox, and I need to talk to someone about it."

"Was it from a dead pigeon pretending it's French, smoking a cigarette and wearing a beret?"

"Yep," Primrose responded, "although I don't know what it's deal with the French is. I had some wonderful times in Paris, and the French were nothing like that—it's an awful stereotype. You got one, too, huh?"

"We all did," Hyacinth answered.

"*All* of you?" Primrose looked back at Mason with a frown. Asking him to handle all five women together would be cruel and unusual punishment. "That's not a good sign."

"It might be," Hyacinth tried to find a positive angle for what was coming as she walked over to the refrigerator. She pulled the number for the cab service she preferred from behind a pizza delivery magnet. After Preston had trashed her car, just like everything else she had ever owned, she decided not to pollute the environment with another one. "Annoying as some of us are, you know we would all die a million times to protect you."

"And you know I would never let that happen," Primrose answered, several books exploding off the shelves behind her at the very thought of it.

"Of course, not, but there's strength in numbers— especially

69

Huxley numbers."

Primrose sighed. "How is the quest for your powers going, Cyn?"

"Not so good," Hyacinth was honest. "I think you're still right about it, though. It's just that I can't ever seem to get past my first Downward Dog without Clover or Iris calling me."

"They're little shits, but they mean well," Primrose replied.

"I know. As a matter of fact, I've got them on the other line right now; Blue, too. I don't think you'll be able to keep us away now."

"With all three of them in on it, I figured as much. Look, I came clean with the Grimms today about the winged rat showing up. They talked to the Council, and everybody agreed that shifting the boundaries to Paradox again for extra protection was a good idea. I need to give you new instructions."

"Shoot," Hyacinth grabbed her notepad and a pen from the kitchen counter. She added, "Fair Warning: Blue will probably insist on bringing her muffins—and Iris already has gas."

"That's all we need to make to this a perfect, reunion. Maybe we should start a butt-plug rule."

"Somebody's feeling adventurous." Mason snuck up behind Prim in time to catch the last sentence. He smacked her on the ass and spoke into the phone, "Sounds like we need to go shopping for you, dirty girl."

"Is that...?" Hyacinth winced.

"Yes, *Hyacinth*," Primrose answered loudly. She rolled her eyes at the well-dressed shifter waiting for an explanation of why she was talking to someone over the phone about sex toys. "The obsessed horn-dog with the exceptionally poor timing is Mason."

"That's horn-*wolf,* not horn-dog," he said.

"Well, tell him hi for me?" Hyacinth asked. "And do your best prepare him for the Huxley Invasion."

"Oh, Goddess!" Primrose thought about the total lack of privacy in the loft upstairs and said goodbye to her peace of mind. "I doubt anyone could do that. Do me a favor and tell the girls you need to bring sleeping bags or blow up mattresses, and linens, okay?"

"Done."

"Blue can share the bed with me. Mason will sleep on one of the mattresses or bags, and I'll trade you if you don't want to sleep on the couch."

"*No.*" Hyacinth was firm. "It's going to be bad enough for him with all of us around. I refuse to let you do that to him. I can take a sleeping bag, and that couch is big and comfy. Blue's not that far along; she should fit on it just fine."

"Tell her she's my favorite already, Rose." Mason wrapped his arms around Primrose's waist and pulled her back against him.

"Cyn," Primrose said and looked up into Mason's face. "You know he's a wolf, right? He's an Alpha, too. Are you going to be okay with him here?"

"I don't know," Hyacinth answered. "I haven't been around another wolf since ... I guess we'll find out when I get there. If it's too bad, I can sleep downstairs in the store."

"You're not kicking her out because of me," Mason frowned. "If somebody needs to sleep downstairs, I'll be the one doing it, Rose."

"He still calls you Rose?" Hyacinth asked.

"Yeah."

"I remember you telling me that a long time ago. I always thought it sounded nice," she sighed. "I've got to get back your incorrigible sisters. Don't worry about the visit, okay? Either one of you—I love you, Prim."

"I love you, too, sis," Primrose said. She gnawed on her lip as she hung up the phone.

"Hey," Mason demanded, tipping her chin to make her look at him. "What's that faraway look on your face about?"

Primrose cleared her throat. "With you being Alpha now, I'm pretty sure there are rules of disclosure about this kind of thing. I need to tell you the whole story about Preston and Hyacinth, including how he died—not just everything he did to her, but what I did to *him*—before my family gets here."

Chapter 12
THE CABBIE

Ipos stared at the 11.5-inch tall, chestnut-haired figure currently sticking out of the cup holder in the vehicle's gray console. *Unbelievable.* That mane-butchering witch had the *gall* to tell him no; Primrose was hidden too well for a locator spell.

Prisma had even claimed he was to blame for not following up on the token his cousin Borana had given to Mason before Primrose negated its magic.

Ipos wasn't an idiot; he understood Intel from a person much closer to his target—specifically, one of the four sisters—had become a necessity. After he had learned the youngest had lost touch with her elemental magic, he certainly agreed that she would be the easiest to ply. So Prisma's offer of a locator spell to find Hyacinth had made sense.

What *didn't* make sense were the taxicab and the locator Barbie—also, the idea that he deserved any part of the blame. This situation was obviously all Borana's fault.

On the other hand, he should have expected something like this. No self-respecting demon wanted anything to do with dolls, and Prisma had the blasted things tucked in cabinets and between swords on the walls of that den of hers.

If carrying a pre-adolescent female's toy weren't bad enough, the miniature version of Hyacinth dressed horrendously. The whole outfit—yoga pants, a t-shirt, and an ugly scarf—offended his sensibilities. He felt an obligation to undo the fashion crime, starting with her shirt.

The bra underneath wasn't bad. It was silky and flesh-colored, with straps and cups sturdy enough to handle the banquet it supported. Sultry black bows rested at the base of each shoulder strap, and a much larger one held court between those magnificent plastic breasts.

The yoga pants weren't doing the doll any favors, either, so off they went. Silky granny panties waited underneath; Ipos wasn't certain how he felt about that. Next, he found the scar under the scarf.

Minor disfigurements weren't a big thing for him.

They shouldn't be; he had caused plenty of them. Prisma said that the damage came from a wolf and Hyacinth felt ashamed of it. In an odd moment of decency, he left the cloth in place.

Her lack of magic aside, he was excited about meeting Hyacinth. No doubt about it, this witch was *womanly*—the delightful antithesis of anorexic girls toys and fashion models. Once someone taught her how to dress all those delightfully dangerous curves, she'd be perfect.

Ipos parked across the street from the gated condominium where the doll's little arm had pointed. He glanced at a beat-up VW van and a few dented sedans nearby and shook his head. A quick glance in the mirror revealed an entirely non-threatening fellow. The floppy hipster hair and chunky glasses practically screamed, "I eat tofu, listen to Radiohead, and believe in world peace."

Keys in hand, he slammed the cab door shut and jogged across the street. There was no traffic, but running seemed somewhat appropriate considering the neighborhood. The metal gate outside her condo was locked; he would have easily gotten past it, ripping it apart in a show of demonic strength, if he hadn't been enjoying all the subterfuge.

"Hello?" Ipos pushed the buzzer on the box and cleared his throat into the speaker. The greeting had come out a little too close to a roar. "Ma'am? Excuse the voice, please. I've got a, um, cold. Ms. Huxley, are you in there? I'm with the cab service."

There was a long pause, and a rustling sound, followed by a soft voice. "You're not Mr.Minassian."

"There's a good reason for that," he answered, trying to think of one.

"But I *asked* for Mr. Minassian," Hyacinth insisted. "I know Mr. Minassian—he's not a stranger."

"Yeah, well," he reminded himself of Step One: Win the witch's trust and get her to unlock the damned gate. "I'm not that strange either; honest. My name's Danny, Danny Chung; something came up for Mr. Minassian at the last minute—family stuff?"

The pause was shorter this time. "Oh, right, I bet it was his grandniece. She's all alone and due any day now."

"Sorry, the old guy left in a blur. No time to go into details. Minassian just asked me to come over as a favor to him, to make sure you get to wherever you're going."

"Alright," Hyacinth responded as the lock on the gate clicked open, "thank you."

The rubber on the bottom of Danny Chung's leather high top dress boots slapped the concrete walkway triumphantly as he approached the condominium.

Smart girl that Hyacinth was, she still hadn't unlocked the front door.

Bang, bang, bang, bang, bang.

"Miss Huxley?" Ipos pounded on the lightly scratched door. A flake of brown paint fell off the upper right corner. "Are you okay in there?"

"Hold on a second."

There was a *snick* as the locking mechanism retreated into the last deadbolt. The door creaked open a bit, as far as a latched chain would allow. She peered at his face over the flimsy metal strand.

"Hi there," Ipos pointed at Hyacinth's last line of defense with a smile. "I think you forgot something."

"Sorry," she answered with a slight self-deprecating laugh. "I'm a bit out of it today, more than usual. It took me the longest time figuring out what to wear."

"No worries," he said, figuring the doll must have had something to do with it. "You know what they say about clothes making the man—or the woman, in this instance."

"Sure." Hyacinth undid the latch. "But I 've never really bought into that whole image thing."

"Maybe you should; it doesn't hurt to dress up every once in a while," Ipos waited for her to open the door and stepped in behind her. She was wearing sweatpants and a matching jacket, along with the scarf. Nothing to write home about, but they fit well enough that he could tell the doll was an accurate depiction.

"Trust me; there's no reason to."

He took a look around. The place was small and sparsely decorated, but she kept it neat inside—if a bit too girlish for his tastes.

"You're *really* a fan of pink, aren't you?"

"No." She handed him a large yellow suitcase with vintage travel stickers all over it. "Personally, I prefer blacks and darker blues; they're more slimming than pastels. Not that I despise pink or anything; it's just that the stuff in here belongs to my landlady."

Ipos shut the front door behind him and set the suitcase beside his feet. He left the thought that Hyacinth shouldn't be slimming down *anything* unspoken. A neatly folded piece of paper clutched in her hand grabbed his attention: Most likely a message from Primrose. The pad and pen she had scrawled it with rested, close by, on the kitchen table.

"Is *that* where I'm dropping you off? Are you going to see this landlady with the pink fetish?"

"Not her," she shook her head. "Somebody else's house, more like family stuff."

"Hey," he said and licked his lips, "I hope you don't think it's presumptuous of me, but I'm feeling kind of thirsty. Do you have anything to drink? Bottled water in the fridge, maybe?"

"No problem." Hyacinth walked past the table to a refrigerator littered with magazine clippings and magnets. *Presumptuous.* The guy had a decent vocabulary for a cabbie. "We all need to hydrate."

Ipos followed behind her, quietly tearing a page from the top of the pad beneath the *clatter* and *swoosh* of the refrigerator's seal giving way. Hyacinth dug inside for two bottles—one for him and one for her. He shoved the indented sheet into an inside jacket pocket and reached for the pen just as she turned around.

"What are you doing?"

"Nothing?"

75

Claw tips emerged from Ipos's fingers. The idea of shredding the sweat suit to find out if her underwear matched the sexiness on the doll held enormous appeal. But that would get him no closer to Primrose *and* lose him a tactical advantage.

"Well, now it's two nothings, Mr. Chung," Hyacinth said as she held out one of the bottles in his direction.

"Excuse me?" He remained clueless, waiting for her to explain.

"First, you try and steal my pen." She held up one finger and changed it to two. "Then, you lie about it. That's not nice. Mr. Minassian would be *greatly* disappointed to know you're treating paying customers this way."

"Oh, sorry." The claws retracted just as covertly as they had surfaced. "It's just that I left mine back at the station."

"You still should have asked," she pointed out, handing him the pen and a bottle, before twisting the cap off her water and taking a swig. "It's the polite thing to do."

"Were you ever a school teacher, by any chance?" Ipos took a small sip from the bottle she offered him. He stashed it in an outside jacket pocket, along with the pen, before walking over to retrieve the yellow case by the door for her.

"A teacher?" Hyacinth grabbed her purse, checking to make sure her cell phone, travel charger, and wallet were all inside. "No, I'm just old-fashioned about most things."

Chapter 13
THE SECRET

Primrose sank into one of the wooden club chairs from the reading nook in the corner. She took a deep breath and closed her eyes, rubbing sweaty palms over its inlaid ivory and coral pattern. Hyacinth was delicate, and Prim wasn't certain being around Mason would help with that. The last thing she wanted was more pain for her youngest sister.

"You don't have to tell me anything, Rose."

"Yes, I do. You seem to be forgetting that you're the one who walked through that door prepared to use Cyn's situation for leverage. Preston's brother is still searching, right? He's not giving up; you said it yourself. Obviously, there's some connection between your pack and his or you wouldn't know about Preston and my sister."

"*Fine*, there is a connection." Mason pulled his chair closer, taking one of her hands in his own. "Preston's sister married a member of my pack. But she's a sweet girl, nothing like either of her brothers. Just let it go for now. We've got more important things to worry about."

"You might not get it yet, but nobody is letting it go," Primrose said. "Wolves aren't that fond of witches to begin with, and Preston's sister is a part of your pack now. Do you honestly imagine you can just *casually* take me as your mate without those worlds colliding?"

"We'll figure it out when this is all through. I'll do damage control on my side, and you can do the same with yours."

"He's dead, Mason—you need to know what happened."

"Then tell me," Mason said as he grabbed both of her hands and forced her to look him in the eyes. "I 'm listening."

"Preston Coleman was an abusive piece of shifter shit. That wolf turned my vibrant, beautiful sister into a fainthearted, apologetic mouse. He beat her and badmouthed her at every turn. Preston deliberately isolated Cyn from anyone who stood a chance at helping her escape."

"From what little his sister has ever said about him, I figured the guy had some serious psychological issues," Mason's replied, his voice gentle.

"No kidding," Primrose snorted, rubbing her eyes beneath the glasses. "He should have been in a mental institution or locked up with a bunch of inmates, not dating Hyacinth."

"You said he isolated her; how did you find out what was going on?"

"He beat her so badly one night that he cracked two of her ribs, and one of her eyes swelled shut."

"*Jesus.*"

"Trust me." Primrose's face was grim. "Jesus had nothing to do with this nasty piece of work. Preston had already trashed her car and taken her phone away. She was in unbearable pain, yet he refused to take her to the doctor; the bastard told her he hoped that she never recovered."

"Please tell me she knows not all wolves are like that."

"We haven't really gotten around to having that conversation; none of us likes to talk about what happened that night. Anyway, Cyn managed to get ahold of Preston's cell phone for long enough to call Blue, and we all went over there together."

"The Huxley avengers," Mason said with a smile. He smoothed a hand over her hair, trying to lighten the mood. "I like the sound of that."

"You won't by the time I get to the end." Primrose shifted in her chair, looking around to ensure there was no one else that might hear them in the aisles of Volumes & Vagaries.

"By the time we got there, it was bad. Preston found out Hyacinth had called, and he was waiting for us in half-wolf form. I don't know what kind of drugs he'd been taking, but he was larger and faster than any wolf we'd ever seen. "

"You think he was on some kind of wolf steroids?"

"I don't know, but what we saw wasn't normal. The only thing that seemed to affect him at all was Iris's fire, but we didn't want to burn the house down, not with Hyacinth still in there."

"Understandable."

"We were all in the thick of it. Clover and Bluebell dodged, and he lunged for me. That's when Cyn came into the room. She could hardly move, but she threw herself in his path to protect me. The claws on one of his hands sliced the front of her neck open like a cantaloupe—my rage over what he had done flipped a switch in me."

"And you're the one who killed him," Mason finished for her. "It's okay, sweetheart. There's no reason to be ashamed. If anyone deserved it, that bastard did. I'd have done the same."

"This is the thing you've got to understand, Mason," she said as she took off her glasses. "What I did to him went beyond murder. It was *desecration.*"

He looked back at her red-rimmed eyes without a word, waiting to hear the rest of the tale.

"This thing inside of me, it turned Preston's entire body inside out. It happened without my working a spell, or even uttering a word. Bones broke, muscles tore, his fur and skin inverted; it was the most violent thing I have ever felt or seen, and I loved every minute of it. My sisters had to watch that monster scream and writhe in agony before he died."

"Well," Mason grimaced and blew out a deep breath. His face was paler than it had been when she started the story, but he wasn't backing down from anything. "That isn't what I *expected* you to tell me, but it's not like he didn't deserve it. What did you do with the body?"

"There wasn't much to do." Primrose placed her glasses back on the bridge of her nose and straightened her spine. "He exploded at the end; Iris incinerated the remains."

"I'll never hear the expression "go out with a bang" without cringing now."

"This isn't funny," she said. "It's *reality.* I desecrated Preston's body. Completely. There is nothing left to return to his brother, even if I wanted to. If his family keeps digging, you're going to have to tell them what happened. There is no way I'm letting anyone's pack punish

Hyacinth for what I've done. I deserve the punishment, not her."

"No one's getting punished," he responded, "and I'm not letting you chase me away just because you're afraid of bonding with me."

"Did you listen to anything I just said? I'm not afraid, Mason; I'm *deadly*." Primrose was desperate for him to understand. "Even if I'm able to handle the stress of a wedding without losing it, how about when you bite me the way you have to, to claim me?"

"I'm not going to lie; it'll probably hurt like hell. You can bite me back. I'll even let you smack me around a bit if you want; I'm completely okay with that. You're worth it."

"Smack you around? Stop being so thick-headed; I could kill you."

"Sweetheart," he responded, pulling her over onto his lap, "as far as I can tell, evil as you think you are, you're only deadly to your enemies. Whatever this power inside of you is—good, bad, or indifferent—it's a part of you. You didn't hurt any of your sisters, and you haven't hurt me. You turned a psychopath inside out. Big deal."

"I've done more than that over the years. There have been times when I wasn't myself."

"I don't care, Rose."

"What about the braless yoga fairy?"

"Is that what we're calling her now?" Mason chuckled. "Well, she was eyeing my package."

"Butt."

"Package, butt, whatever—it's all *yours*, and she clearly wanted to get her sneaky little handprints all over it."

"Goddess," she shook her head, smacking him in the arm, "what did I ever do to deserve such an arrogant, conceited man?"

"You were the most beautiful woman I had ever seen."

"Aside from Brunhilde. Or Borana. Or whatever we're calling the super sexy Succubus these days," Primrose reminded him as the phone at the front desk rang.

"It's a good thing you're gorgeous—because you're not funny at *all*." He wrapped his arms tight around her and planted a kiss on her cheek before letting her go.

Primrose sprinted to the front desk and picked up the phone. "Hello? You've reached Volumes & Vagaries. "

"Prim?" Hyacinth was hesitant. Primrose could hear Clover and Iris chatting in the background; Blue told them to zip it. "We're all together, and we're on our way. It will probably be a couple of hours or so, based on the directions for finding the closest boundary."

"No problem," Primrose said. The instructions to the crossroads were always cryptic. Asking the Council to change its ways was useless; it was a fairy thing. "We'll be expecting you. What's wrong, Hyacinth? Something's up; I can hear it in your voice."

"I had a new cab driver," Hyacinth sighed. "I'd never seen him before. He said Mr. Minassian had an emergency and asked him to pick me up instead as a favor," Hyacinth sighed. "Mr. Minassian doesn't employ outsiders. Bluebell got a bad feeling from inside the house. At least, he didn't see her baby bump when he dropped me off."

"You're okay, though, right? He didn't try to hurt you, did he?"

"No," she responded. "He just came inside the condo and asked for water. Seemed like a decent guy although he was a total hipster. At first, I thought maybe he had a daughter; there was a Barbie doll in the console next to him but more like real girl dimensions. Bigger everything."

"We all know of someone who uses dolls in her magic," Bluebell spoke loudly enough from Primrose to hear, "and we haven't heard from her for quite some time. Almost *too* long."

"Hard to forget Gran," Primrose said, "since she's the other reason for my predicament. Kind of weird she surfaces just when Ipos is looking for me, too, isn't it? Somehow, I doubt she's with us in all of this."

"Which means..." Bluebell added.

"Told you!" Iris shouted. "Gran-Gran is always *against us*, so you can stop being such a stupid dildo and holding onto hope for her, Clover!"

Chapter 14
THE INVASION

"So this is Mr. Wolfy Pants, the love 'em and leave 'em guy, huh?"

Clover gave Mason the once over. Her expression clearly said two things: I don't care much for shifters, and I don't give a shit about the size of your anything, you hairy bastard.

"Yep," Iris answered, handing the smartly attired man in question her suitcase along with Bluebell's, "but he totally gets a break on that love 'em and leave 'em thing, Clover—because he returned. That's *un-leaving*."

"Thank you." Mason reserved hope that the two sisters might discover the beauty of their indoor voices upstairs in what was going to be an incredibly cramped loft. "And I also appreciate *you* giving me the benefit of the doubt, Clover."

"That's funny because I don't recall saying that I was going to give you anything."

"You know better than to challenge a wolf, Clover," Bluebell sighed, shaking her head as she walked past. She rubbed her belly and complained about having to pee before following the signs to the downstairs bathroom reserved for customers.

"I don't know," Clover shrugged. "The last wolf I challenged didn't fare so well."

"What happened to him had nothing to do with you," a soft voice corrected her, "and you know Prim and I prefer that you not talk about it, Clover."

"Sorry, Cyn." Clover looked as guilty as a dog caught tearing into the next-door neighbor's trash.

"You must be Hyacinth," Mason offered the curvy woman a warm smile. "It's a pleasure to meet you. Rose shared what happened with me; I'm so sorry."

"Well," Iris said, "the wolf's out of the bag now, kids!"

"I hope you don't mind. She wanted to make sure you girls were still comfortable—that includes not having to worry about what you say around me."

"Oh," Clover interjected, "you mean like how you shouldn't be calling us girls because we're grown women? And her nickname's *Prim*, not Rose."

"*Girl*, please!" Iris snorted at her. "You call me that all the time. You're just being bitchy because he's got a penis and you don't think it's good enough for Prim. Seriously, Mason, don't mind her. Clover's all bat shit crazy and possessive. Also, she's probably threatened by your wolf dong."

"Don't call me bat shit *anything*," Clover snapped back at her, "you vampire loving, male genitalia obsessing..."

"Oh, no," Primrose groaned as she came around the corner. "Please tell me you're not talking about Mason's penis already, Iris."

Already? Mason raised an eyebrow at Primrose but kept his mouth shut. It was only day one of the dreaded Huxley Invasion, after all.

"Okay, girls." Primrose didn't bother acknowledging how over-the-top crazy any of the usual weirdness must seem to an outsider. It was true what they said about picking friends and being stuck with family. On the bright side, none of these women would ever die on her. "Mason, would you mind watching the front desk for me while we go upstairs and have a chat?"

The look of relief on Mason's face was enough to assure them all that he didn't mind one bit.

"Sorry," Bluebell said as Clover and Iris marched up the stairs with her bags in hand. "We are a handful. Don't feel obligated to lie and say that we're not; it's okay."

"For what it's worth." Hyacinth said, hanging behind for a moment after Blue had gone, "she didn't mean to do it."

"Which one?" Mason realized he wanted to see this sister smile just as much as Rose did. "Clover didn't mean to insult me? Or Iris didn't mean to mention my unmentionables?"

"I was talking about Prim," she laughed, "and I can see why she finds you so charming. I'm assuming if she told you everything that you know about the power inside of her and what the demon did to wake it up."

"I do," he nodded. "But I don't believe that power defines her any more than you do."

"We're an odd couple, Prim and me," Hyacinth admitted. She paused for a moment, looking down at her hands. "One of us is terrified of what she might become; the other is so numb she can't seem to figure out why she even exists. You have to understand: She may doubt herself, but we don't. Prim would never pose a threat to those she loves—she only kills monsters."

"We're already on the same page where my Rose is concerned, little sister."

"Good. That makes you family, as far as I'm concerned."

"Oh, and Hyacinth?" Mason asked as the youngest Huxley turned to head for the stairs.

"Yeah?"

"You sisters are right about you, you know."

"Right how?"

"You're a beautiful, valuable woman. It doesn't matter whether you get your powers back or not. The actions of a tyrant and all the ugly words in the world can't change who you are; just how you feel."

"Thanks." Mason could hear her tears though she had already turned away. "That's very kind of you—I promise never to call you Wolfy Pants."

"Greatly appreciated," he answered. "Don't tell anyone I said so, but you're officially my favorite. Go upstairs, the troops are waiting—and leave the bags; I'll bring them. Tell Rose if we don't have any customers in the next hour, I'm closing the shop and coming upstairs to see what's going on. Mrs. Grimm is the only one who comes around this time of day, anyway."

"You're a brave man, Mason Géroux."

"Or a foolish one!" he called after Hyacinth as he watched her walk away. "I know that's what you're thinking!"

Hyacinth walked down the far aisle toward the stairs. She hummed softly, inhaling the familiar, welcoming scents of books and dust. Hard as it was to get to, it was impossible not to love Volumes & Vagaries. She was still grateful for Prim's obtaining permission for her to stay and recover in safety and peace the first few months after Preston's death.

For those clever enough to crack the code, crossing fairies boundaries without permission was still a serious transgression. The only reason Primrose had gotten away with it when she arrived was her refusal to defend herself against the Grimms. The two principal sentinels for Paradox had sensed how powerful she was, and they respected that.

Hyacinth paused for a moment on the stairs, remembering the big black cat in the back alley. *King.* The tomcat had been beautiful and harmless—the farthest thing from a wolf—and the two of them had gotten along famously.

Maybe King was still around. Hopefully, Mason's presence here hadn't chased him away. She'd have to ask Prim about it later, once all the craziness with Ipos blew over.

Chapter 15
THE RIDDLE

"This is why I've always hated the Fae—flighty, cryptic little bastards, always speaking in stupid riddles."

Ipos handed over the top sheet from the notepad to punctuate his complaint. He had already colored it in with the pen Hyacinth caught him trying to steal, but the message made no sense.

"Flighty, I can't argue with," Prisma replied, "but little is a misnomer. They come in an astounding variety of sizes. Stupid is wrong, as well. In my experience, all of their puzzles and gambits are highly intelligent—and so is my granddaughter for aligning herself with the Grays."

"How do you know it's the Grays?"

"The rest of the Fae are too full of themselves, and their own politics, to help."

Prisma placed the paper on an elaborate roll topped desk with a gigantic, brass keyhole. A plaque on the side said it belonged to someone long dead and famous. It wasn't that impressive; the magic had helped substantially with his fame.

She considered the five phrases that the pen's ink had revealed thoughtfully:

—Spare the oak and spoil the ash.

—There is too much thyme on your Hans.

—This is truly no mourning for glories.

—Leave them behind and travel lightly.

—Do it with your shins.

"Spare the oak and spoil the ash, " Prisma tackled the statements in sequential order. "That sounds like a play on "spare the rod and spoil the child." Oak, ash and thorn are a sacred trio for them."

Ipos assumed they were talking about faeries, not random disciplinarians.

"So are we looking for a clearing with just oak and ash trees or oak, ash, and thorn?"

"You're already getting ahead of yourself," the witch pointed out with a shake of her head. "There's no certainty it's even trees that we're talking about yet."

"Those are kinds of trees," he said, "and we're wasting precious time deliberating."

"Yes, but remember why you hate the fairies."

"There are fifty million reasons to hate them, and you are quickly becoming one of them. What are we looking for, if not types of wood, Prisma?"

"I told you, we don't know; the words merely serve as clues."

"I should gut you, woman," Ipos sneezed violently. "And stop burning incense in here! The air is already teeming with allergens."

Prisma pursed her lips, wondering if he was going to mention King's fur, too. It was bad enough when paying customers whined incessantly about everything; Ipos's bellyaching was intolerable.

"It's my den, and I'll do what I want. That includes filling it, from wall to wall, with all the things that make you itch. You're rather fragile for a monster; less of a lion, more of a great, big pussycat, arent you?"

"Don't be rude."

"Deal with it. Or stop trying to order me around like a child. You need me more than I need you—so mind the misogyny, dear."

"What is it with everyone calling me a misogynist?"

"Fine; call yourself the King of Denial, instead. Not my concern—just be nice while you're under my roof. Once our business ends, and that love spell I made goes to work on its intended target, you're welcome to say and do whatever the hell you want."

"Whatever I want in Hell," he corrected her.

"That's your habitat; not mine, dear." Prisma would turn his tail to ice and break it off before allowing their conversation to devolve into the juvenile, demonic version of adding in bed to the end of every statement. "Why don't you play with some of my dollies, or stare at something shiny, while I continue to work on this puzzle?"

"I hate those dolls, and you need to watch the condescension," Ipos responded with a flash of claws. "Stop talking down to me before I have to teach you some respect, woman."

"I'm a witch, not a woman, where you're concerned," she enunciated with a flash of teeth as he stood. "And, as we have already established, I'm the one doing the teaching, demon. Unless you prefer to go back to deciphering riddles on your own?"

"Oh for Lucifer's sake," he sat down again. "Go ahead."

"Let's assume Thyme indicates the actual herb. Hans is mostly likely a reference to Hans Christian Anderson—after all, the man put a dozen fairy stories into books."

"Weren't the fairies enraged over their secrets being divulged by the man?"

"Yes, you remember correctly; not all of them were happy about the press—but not all of what he wrote was true, either. The royal courts on both sides, the dark and the light, eventually came to a stalemate on the matter and agreed to let it go."

"And he wrote more than a dozen stories."

"No argument from me, there, Mr. Know It All. The man was a prolific author, no doubt. I was speaking in general terms, though. Faeries create riddles that are tricky—tricky but never unfathomable. Therefore, we can stick with his most famous pieces, which might even be less than a dozen: Little Mermaid, Ugly Duckling, Emperor's New Clothes, Nightingale that kind of thing."

"What nightingale?" he asked. "I don't remember that one."

"An Emperor learns that the nightingale's song is the most beautiful sound in his kingdom. He spurns the real bird for an extravagant mechanical one that has been gifted to him. The toy eventually breaks. As he lays dying, the real nightingale comes back, sings for him, and its song restores him."

"That is both boring and stupid," Ipos moved on. "What about the "mourning for glories" line?"

"Could be the flower," Prisma said, "providing mourning was intended as a homonym. Or it might be a place where glory is a thing of the past due to genuine mourning: a cemetery."

"Travel lightly; do it with your shins?" the demon asked.

"Easy enough; Widdershins means counter-clockwise."

"Isn't that unlucky?"

"Well, yes, but the rules of travel are quirky and, frankly, when you're crossing over one of their boundaries uninvited, anything and everything is unlucky. The direction in which you move is the least of your worries, you fool."

Ipos growled and stalked over to a sword on the wall. Prisma's magic radiated from it. He could touch the instrument, feel the contours of the blade, and even stroke the jewels and patterned hilt. He could probably cut all of his fingers off with it; what he couldn't do was take it down and use it on her.

"Is this thing a replica of Charlegmagne's sword?"

"No," Prisma replied. "That thing you are getting your nasty fingerprints all over is the original. The Louvre has a replica."

"And this other one with all the big lettering?"

"Belonged to Ivan the Terrible—but he wasn't that bad, to be honest."

"You don't happen to have the Hope Diamond around here, do you? I might have a use for it."

"Sorry," she replied. "The only cursed jewelry I've ever been in the market for is the piece you're giving back to me. The Hope Diamond is still at the Smithsonian."

"How did you get your hands on all these artifacts?"

"My girlish charms?" she responded, batting her eyelashes in his direction.

"Try again," Ipos commanded.

"I'm highly resourceful. Aside from that, it's none of your beeswax."

"What if I decided to make it my beeswax?" Ever the bully, he pushed back.

"If you tell me every last one of your weaknesses, I might consider it. Other than that, prepare to be stung. Try learning by any other means, and you'll have no success with the potion I'm giving you today. No love for the mighty prince. All my work—the spells and the potions—come with what I like to call Prisma Insurance."

"Meaning?"

"It's all in the fine print, dear. The maker of said spells reserves the unequivocal right to revoke her magic—at any time, for any reason. Translation: Be nice. Play nice. *Stay* nice."

"Of course," he answered, "I intend to be nice to you, my dearest, darling Prisma. Cross my heart and hope you die."

"You and damned near every Huxley on the planet," she chuckled, squinting her eyes at him. The fuzzy reprobate could be quite charming when trying to pretend he could pull off any sort of plan without her help. "And that's a very, very long list, so you'll just have to get in line behind all of them."

"A pity I don't do lines," he responded, twisting his neck sharply in the direction of a door that had opened and shut, by itself, with a slam, "they're beneath me. Tell me, Prisma, is there anything else I need to be concerned about here?"

"Probably not," Prisma smirked, not bothering to look up from the riddle this time. She was on the cusp of having the answer. Let the sharp-tempered demon be nervous; it was good for his character.

"Why?"

"Stored in one central location like this, magical items build up a massive amount of energy over time. Everyone once in a while they need to blow off steam."

"That sounds a lot like "shit happens," Ipos said.

"Invariably, it does. Now, if you promise to be a good little demon who knows not to question my authority, I'll tell you a lot more than that."

"You've figured it out?"

"Yes, you impetuous imp, I believe I have."

"Then let's get going," the demon responded, reaching for her hand.

"That is not how this is going to work," Prisma leaned back and stared at his hand as if he'd just asked her to scrub toilets. "I have a business to run, and that business currently has little to do with an obsessive demon on a power binge."

"You stand to benefit, or you wouldn't be helping me at all, my dear."

"Truer words have never been spoken," Prisma agreed, getting on with the business of signs and what to do once he spotted them.

Somewhere near the neighborhood where he had dropped Hyacinth off, Ipos would look for a combination of things. First, there should be a large statue or structure made of oak and ash—the ash was the lighter wood. Second, wild thyme and morning glories would congregate at the base. Third, there should be a rack or a shelf protruding from the thing— something large enough to accommodate a coat. After leaving his coat as an offering, he would need to walk around the entire thing counter clockwise.

"For how long?" he asked.

"Do I look like a psychic to you? I don't know, you idiot; just do it until you notice a change of scenery."

"Those cryptic little bastards are not getting my good coat," Ipos overlooked the insult. He was more concerned with obtaining some backup and a spare outer garment first.

Chapter 16
THE INTEL

Auntie Golem handed the harpy, whose pedicure she had just finished, a buy one *gris-gris*, get one free coupon for the voodoo queen around the corner. She pushed her out the door of the Better Than The Ones In Your Coffin nail salon and turned to Borana.

"I have a lead on the identity of the TLS contact, but you're not going to like it, Bubula."

"Not going to like it, huh? Big whoop." Borana did her best golem imitation, picking up a tube of peppermint scrub and a bottle of clear coat. She slapped them onto the counter along with her credit card. "We both know I have never liked anything to do with the Schlemiel in the first place. Ring me up, and tell me the tale."

The golem typed in the actual value of the two items. She looked up at Borana, quoting a ridiculously small figure.

"That can't be right," the Succubus said, cocking a lush eyebrow. "Come on, Auntie. We're never going to get you to retirement this way; add two more zeros, I insist."

"Now I know what they mean about those legendary powers of seduction." The golem cracked a rare smile. "Retirement: It's my one weakness. You're supposed to pay once and refer future business, girlie. Leave it to you to figure out how to ply me with hope."

"It's not selfless; this is all quid pro quo." Borana gave her a wink. "Eventually, one of our lives is going to get better. Naturally, I figured your chances were probably better than mine, so why not help a golem out?"

"I thought demons were supposed to cause misery and suffering."

"I thought golems didn't have personalities."

"Touché," Auntie Golem said.

"Not that anyone believes I'm telling the truth," Borana responded with a shrug, "but I'm capable of leading an army. That should be worth some suffering and misery, right?"

"Absolutely."

"By the way, if I ever gain control of all my assets, I want you to come live with me at the castle. Forget retirement; we'll buy you this place, and you can be a hands and feet mogul."

"You're a talented gal, and I'm proud to call you my pretend niece. These old wooden legs will cut a rug at your wedding if you ever get around to having one. Now, hand over that credit card before you change your mind."

"Yes, Ma'am." Borana saluted. "And please spill the golem beans."

"So," Auntie Golem said as she swiped the card again, "it just so happens that the wraith with the war pigeons knows a Poltergeist that travels in a suitcase."

Borana chewed on her bottom lip, "I never have any idea where you are going with these stories."

"It's called suspense; take a seat and get used to it."

Borana sank into one of the cushy chairs meant to lull clientele. "Sitting doesn't mean I'm asking you to work, but go ahead."

"You're growing on me girl; don't stop." The golem eyeballed her before resuming the tale. "This poltergeist suitcase that the pigeon wrangler happens to know briefly ended up in the hands of a Bohemian retiree who ended up in a bed and breakfast being run by a Huxley."

"Seriously? Which witch was it?"

"The grandma, Prisma. You can only tell by the names since these bitches—excuse me, *witches*—don't age."

"I don't age either, and I don't hear you calling me a bitch," Borana defended Primrose and Clover—mostly Clover.

"Yeah, well, you're from Hell; that's different. So, as I was saying, this bed and breakfast was owned by the granny, and the poltergeist left the suitcase and took a stroll around the grounds because it felt a lot of witch juice."

"Okay."

"Want to guess where it ended up?"

"I have no idea," Borana said, leaning forward in the leather salon chair.

"Do you want to know?"

"Of course, I do! Spit it out before I shred this chair to pieces and ruin my manicure!"

"Sorry," Auntie Golem said. "I was building suspense. It's the sign of all great storytellers, the suspense thing."

"Pretty please with demonic sugar on top, Auntie Golem, just tell me where this ghost went and what it saw."

"It ended up in some secret room none of the other guests can access. There were all kinds of weird, dark magic paraphernalia on the walls, too: swords, and dolls, and whatnot. Not too long after that, Prisma Huxley came in with a French guy. He turned out to be your cousin in disguise."

"Wait!" Borana held up her nails in disbelief. "You're saying Ipos's expert in the field is a HUXLEY?"

"Not just a Huxley, *the* Huxley; the one who traded a piece of Primrose's soul for some locket in the first place. Ipos is giving the necklace back to her in return for her help, and it only gets worse from there."

"Go on."

"Apparently, she's not only figured out how to find Primrose. The witch also made him a pretty powerful love potion in trade."

"Fan-*freaking*-tastic!" The Succubus rolled her dark eyes at the news. "I give Primrose her mate back and lose my shot with Clover, all for nothing—because now the Lion Schlemiel is getting a love potion?"

"Your shot was fercockt to begin with; these are cursed witches," Auntie Golem said. "Some old Mesopotamian shtick to repay the original Huxley hussy for banging somebody she shouldn't have. Now, to paraphrase Johnny Mercer, something's always got to give. At least, where luck or love comes into play."

"That sucks."

"Yeah, but it *did* give me a great idea for merchandising, depending on how things go. What do you think about 'Glad I'm Not A Huxley' t-shirts?"

"The idea is tasteless and completely insensitive. It's instant pop culture."

"Pop culture! That is exactly what I'm talking about," the golem said, nodding enthusiastically. "If nobody's patented the idea, I could work with local vendors. Get the right demons to wear my stuff, and that might be what makes me my fortune. I could pay for that retirement, a cabana boy, and then some. You could live with me!"

"Just don't expect me to buy one."

"No offense, but I don't think you've ever worn a t-shirt in your life."

"It's not my fault," Borana said. "Casual attire took on a different meaning for me during the formative years. My mother had my little red butt in leopard-print diapers from day one."

"Are you sure you're a lesbian?"

"Yes, and I don't even own a pair of Birkenstocks; *now* look who's falling back on stereotypes."

"Clit for tat, Bubula," the golem said.

"Ugh. I should have known. You're willing to go a long way for a pun, aren't you?"

"It's called showmanship, and, yes, I am."

"So what am I going to do about this love spell, when I can't even find the girls to warn them?"

"Well," the golem said, tapping at a decorative wart carved into her chin, "where did you last see this Clover of yours?"

"Kingdom Come," Borana replied. "It's a club topside; fun place, not a lot of rules. The bar inside is the one we met at."

"Sounds like the best place to start, then. Go home and grab your dancing shoes; you need to find out how well people know her there."

"She's unbelievably cocky." Borana grinned. "We're talking about the confidence of a charging bull, in a hall with wall-to-wall red curtains. I'm pretty sure just about everything with a vagina there has known her at some point."

"Find out which one knows her best and take it from there."

"Will do, Auntie Dearest!" Borana gave her a two-fingered salute before she and her small bag of expensive salon products marched out of the door.

CHAPTER 17
THE ANGEL

"Sorry," Borana apologized for the crack her sexual kung fu left in the fountain at Kingdom Come.

The little marble lady didn't seem to mind. The fact that the statue's response came in a much deeper voice than usual made her wonder if the club owner linked his consciousness to it. Or maybe it had always been the gargoyle in disguise, and he had some voyeuristic bent. Either way, she didn't see how his kinks were any of her concern.

Borana sidled over to the bar. She took a long way, weeding through the crowd with a wicked smile for every set of eyes that ogled her. The top of her white leopard-print club dress with the floor length skirt consisted of two silky strips forming an X in the front; it barely covered her nipples. The strips tied neatly together behind her neck, leaving the lines of her back exposed. On the bottom half, a slit ran high up the side of one nicely muscled thigh.

House techno pumped hard and fast in the air around her, and neon reflections from the dance floor followed in her wake. So did the handful of dancers that noticed her, leaving confused partners on the floor. They couldn't help it; her pheromones made her the most interesting thing in the room.

As Borana approached the busy bar, some variety of shifter—she couldn't quite tell what from the eyes or the smell—offered her his stool. She accepted with a smile, then shooed him away with a wink and the truth.

Lesbian.

The bartender glanced in her direction and did a double take that told her he remembered. He finished with his last customer and walked over.

"You want another Screaming Orgasm?"

"Wouldn't be the same without you-know-who," she said, shaking her head. "You don't happen to know where she is, do you?"

"Nope; sorry."

"Then I'll take a martini, straight up with a twist of lime."

"That's about as far away from an orgasm as girls like you get, isn't it?" a sweet voice posed the question on her left.

Borana shifted to consider a caramel-skinned female with smoky eyes and a surprisingly demure lace gown. The implication of the dress was somewhere between ballerina and bride, the exact opposite of what anyone might expect to see in Kingdom Come.

"You're right about that," she said, keeping her movements gentle and slow as she offered a hand in greeting. "My name's Borana; I'm guessing you already know that."

"I suppose our Intel is legendary." The female nodded in return, taking the Succubus's hand. She shivered a little and let go. "It's nice to meet you, Borana. My name is Angelíta."

"Kind of a cliché, isn't it?" Borana chuckled as the bodies began backing away from the two of them. Even *she* had to admit that it was a little odd to see a demon and an angel chatting each other up.

"It might be," the angel replied, "but the name was mine long before I became an angel, *dama demonio*. I'm here because we heard you were interested in helping the Huxley witches."

Lady Demon? Hilarious; she hadn't been called a lady in ages. "Just out of curiosity, does this collective *we* consider helping the Huxley brood a good or a bad thing these days?"

"Good."

"Fabulous!" Borana responded, signaling the bartender, "Between you, me, and, apparently, all of Heaven, I could really use the help. Let me buy you a drink."

"Oh, no, thank you," Angelíta said. "My superiors mentioned I should never let you ply me with alcohol."

"That'll be water, then?" the bartender asked.

"Yes, please."

"No way," Borana amended the order, "make that a wine spritzer with Gewürztraminer, please."

The angel stared.

"Don't worry, Angel Cake, there's an entire ounce of club soda in this. Live a little—you can still tell them, in all honesty, that you drank fizzy water around the evil temptress when they grill you about it."

"I'm not certain..." Angelíta responded.

"That you should trust her?" A gravelly baritone intruded from the other side of the heavenly Latina.

"Precisely," the angel turned, looking up at a gigantic mountain of muscular stone in a pinstriped suit, "and this place isn't exactly Sunday School to begin with."

"God forbid," the gargoyle responded. "No offense intended. It's just that I gave up the hanging out on the rooftops business a long, long time ago. If this place were a chapel, I'd never turn a profit."

"No offense taken." Angelíta decided to be polite about it.

The gargoyle nodded to his bartender. "Take that drink and enjoy it, honey. The name's Mac; I own this place, and I'd like to invite you two lovely ladies into my private booth. You can talk without anyone eavesdropping, and I'll hang around to vouch for your angelic safety."

"Do I want to know why you're being so generous?" Borana asked dryly.

"Clover Huxley is a long-term patron of Kingdom Come," he said, smiling as innocently as a rock could. "That makes her a friend of mine."

"And?" Borana thought about the deal with the statue at the entrance; she wasn't buying the unsullied explanation.

"And that *other* thing, too." His look said it all; he knew she had no moral grounds to stand on.

"*What* thing?" the angel in lace frowned, looking back and forth between the two of them.

The gargoyle kept his trap shut.

Borana asked the other female about her experience with the statue before coming in.

"I gave it my blessing."

"Anything else?"

"The wind blew my skirt up."

"Yep," Borana answered, smacking her lips loudly for emphasis, "that would be Clover's power—her contribution to this whole, weird evening."

"Weird how?" The angel still wasn't quite getting it.

"I see and feel everything the fountain does," the gargoyle rumbled, watching Angelíta's face with an angel-eating grin. "Take my advice and ditch those granny panties; your ass is too good for them. Invest in some hipsters, maybe a few nice pairs of boy shorts, instead.

"You should never address an angel about her underwear." Angelíta was horrified.

"I feel that doing hundreds of years worth of time for your people in Italy entitles me to speak my mind."

"I'm not *Italian*," the angel replied. "My family came from Mexico—I grew up in Los Angeles."

"I didn't mean *your people* like that." He looked horrified. "I was referring to your employers: the whole upstairs crowd."

"Oh, my apologies. It's hard to tell if you're being derogatory. Your voice has so little inflection."

"Granite vocal cords, babe—among other things."

Borana rolled her eyes, a cocktail glass in each hand. "Are you still down for this whole booth-conversation thing, oh holy one?"

"Yes; I have no choice *but* to be ready. I'm acting on orders, and there are things you need to know."

The crowd parted for the three of them, allowing passage to an alcove in the back corner of the bar. It was a secluded spot, roped off with red velvet and hidden by heavily lined black and white curtains. The fabric had repeating martini glasses and a list of all two of Kingdom Come's

Commandments.

"Ladies first." Mac pulled back the curtains, and ushered them in.

Borana slid into a red leather bench that showcased her dress on the right of a rich mahogany table. Angelíta's internal debate was evident as she looked from the red seat to the white one on the opposite side.

"Promise not to touch?" the angel finally asked.

"Nope!" the gargoyle winked.

"Yes," Borana said.

The two females settled in across from him, and the gargoyle closed the curtains and signaled them to get started.

"The Huxley Curse is ancient and powerful," Angelíta began, "I'm sure you already know that part; it's what makes the Huxley line so legendary. A Mesopotamian Queen—the title for a Queen was *eresh* in the language of the day—initiated it."

Mac casually stretched across the table as the angel spoke. He extended his fingers in an attempt to remove the thin strips of material covering Borana's nipples.

Borana slapped his hands away. "Watch it with the fingers, Rock Face!"

"What?" he responded, "Look at you; it's semantics at this point. Think about it—if you let the girls loose here, behind the curtain, poor Angelíta could stop stressing about whether or not they'll fall out."

Angelíta muttered something that had *dios* in it and continued with the story.

The ancient queen was quite beautiful and powerful. She had a husband and a lover, and her lover was the handsomest man in all the land—on a scale of 1-10, this guy was a 12.5. One day, the handsome lover met a witch who was even prettier than the queen. The two of them, the witch and the lover, fell in love and ran away together.

"And that was Huxley Witch, Version 1.0," Borana said.

"Exactly."

Angelíta continued with the story, explaining how the wicked queen couldn't let the insult go. She hunted the couple down, killed the man, and commanded thirteen sorcerers at her disposal to devise a suitable revenge for the witch's sin. Only, in this instance, the couple's messing around hadn't been a sin. Despite the man having already been the queen's paramour, he was the ancestral Huxley witch's one true love.

"That explains why Clover Huxley used to hang out here all the time," Mac said. "If you can't get romance, you might as well get laid. You know, something to fill the void."

"That's surprisingly insightful of you." The angel seemed surprised.

"I've got something powerful we could use to fill *your* void. Borana can even warm you up. I'll just sit over here like a good boy until she's through with you, I promise."

"Charming, but no, from both of us." Borana shared a look with the angel. "Lechery isn't going to solve the Huxley problem. Angelíta, all you've laid out for us so far is backstory. Why me, and how does any of this help save Primrose from my cousin's clutches?"

"Believe it or not, you have the potential for good. Plus, you're already in with Clover, and beggars can't be choosers. Ipos is a hopeless jerk, hungry for unstoppable power. No one on my side wants that. Also, he's being manipulated by the curse, whether he realizes it or not."

"Makes sense," Borana agreed, "but this is going to be tough. The PI I'm working with—*okay*, she's more of a golem in a nail salon—told me Ipos just went to the girls' grandmother for help. Prisma made him a love potion in return for the locket responsible for screwing Primrose up in the first place."

"That's messed up," the gargoyle rumbled. "I guess he figured it takes one to get one, though."

"Guess so," the Succubus took a sip of her drink and drummed her fingers on the table. "So, tell me, how am I going to battle this thing?"

"First, don't be so quick to judge their grandmother," Angelíta answered, "and, second, by 'this' do you mean the curse?"

"No, I mean my yeast infection," Borana responded, watching the club owner cringe. "Not so sexy after that, now, am I?"

"My junk's carved out of stone." He thought about it and didn't care. "It's not like I'm catching anything by taking a trip down there."

"You're disgusting." Angelíta had to say it.

"That's so sweet, you thinking a hunk of rock like me has feelings. Forget about it and get on with the enlightenment, Dali Labia."

"Don't you mean Dali Lama?"

"Do you keep him between your legs?"

"We start with damage control," the angel sighed and chugged down half of her spritzer in one gulp.

"Ending the curse for the entire bloodline is a long-term goal. It would be spectacular PR with the pagan community, but we have no idea how; every soul that had a hand in creating it appears to have been wiped from existence. Frankly, we haven't even identified the force on the other end of Prisma's bargain yet."

"So you're just as clueless," Borana said with a frown. "How can Heaven *and* Hell not know?"

"That's not something I lose sleep over. It's too far above my pay grade. In answer to your other question—how we intend to battle things— we're thinking much smaller here."

Borana pointed to the granite figure across from them, "How much teensier are you thinking? Like his *penis* or my pinkie?"

"Evil demon, making a molehill out of a mountain," Mac chuckled. "Trust me, I look forward to proving just how wrong Miss Succu-Boobs is to you, my sweet, tasty Angelíta. We won't even let her watch, not unless she asks very nicely."

"Uh-huh, whatever." Borana glared at him, then burst out laughing as she picked up on the energy coming off the lovely Latina with the disapproving face. "Wait, I take that back, Rock Boy. You may be on to something here."

"I mean smaller *as in* there's a person you need to see, to intervene with Primrose and set you on your path. Right after you call Clover's cell number, which the folks upstairs said I could give you, to warn her."

Angelíta held it together, despite a beet red face and the desire to crawl under the table. "You two are *highly* inappropriate; I could lose my job for this."

"Let me guess." A light bulb suddenly came on in Borana's head. "You were the stripper with a heart of gold who died committing some courageous act?"

"Totally irrelevant how it happened." The angel slugged the last of her spritzer.

"Looks like you ladies need another round!" Mac responded to the revelation joyously, a picture of Angelíta dancing on the table now lodged in his head. "Something stronger on the house this time. I insist on it!"

CHAPTER 18
THE CALL

"Hang on a minute." Everyone stared at Clover, who apparently had no problem pausing mid-argument with Iris to answer her cell phone. "Yell-oh?"

"I thought Paradox didn't allow unauthorized signals to get through?" Bluebell glanced over at Primrose expectantly.

"Yeah, but she's all kinds of whorish." Iris cupped one hand into a loose circle and slid her index finger in and out suggestively. "Maybe she did some Gray finger-banging with one of your neighbors for special privileges."

Hyacinth stopped unpacking in the corner opposite Prim's sparring equipment. She did it for just long enough to cover her face and shake her head sadly. Iris had always been the Huxley idiot savant, minus the savant part.

"Borana, hey!" The whole room watched Clover's posture shift from bitch to interested in record time. "I didn't expect to hear from you, woman. No, I'm not complaining. As a matter of fact, it's awesome! How did you get my number?"

Primrose and Mason shared a wide-eyed glance at the sound of the Succubus's name. What was she doing calling Clover?

"A girl at Kingdom Come?" Clover grimaced and crossed her fingers. "Did she say anything good about me? No, no, you're right. It doesn't matter. What can I do to you? Sorry, Freudian slip; I meant *for* you."

Surprising everyone but Mason, Primrose snapped and grabbed the phone from Clover's hand. "Borana? Yes, hi, this is *Primrose*. What kind of game are you playing with my sister? Is this about Mason again?"

Against everyone's recommendation, Clover rushed at an equally agitated eldest sister in an attempt to retrieve her property. She found herself shoved back across the room by a sudden burst of power.

Primrose nodded, listening with brief interjections for several minutes before she tossed the phone back to a über-pissed Clover. Borana's suggestion that Clover ask her sister what was going on before they said goodbye did nothing to improve her mood.

"Why is my future girlfriend talking to you, and what's it got to do with *him*?" Clover demanded, stabbing an adamant finger in Mason's direction.

"Just calm down, you guys." Hyacinth did her best to intercede. "Please?"

"Oh, for Goddess's sake." Primrose stared back at her stubborn, green-haired sibling in disbelief. "What is *wrong* with you? She is a Succubus!"

Bluebell excused herself, shuffling off to the other side of the loft. She mumbled something about needing to use the toilet, asking them to hold off on any and all murder attempts until she came back into the room.

"Got it, Blue!" Iris responded for everyone. She offered two thumbs up, showing off her black nail polish before lifting herself up onto the kitchen counter for a better view.

"She's more than some demon to me!" Clover shrieked. "Now, you tell me what is going on here, Primrose *Halldora* Huxley!"

Mason glanced over at Hyacinth. The brunette nodded, mouthing the name Halldora in silent confirmation. Prim was fairly certain she would never hear the end of it.

Primrose took off her glasses. She rubbed her eyes and asked herself what she had done to deserve this much chaos and calamity. The answer was clear as ever: She had been born a freaking Huxley.

"I will," Prim responded, reminding Clover that Blue had asked them to wait.

"Technically it was only on the murder part." Iris gnawed the paint from the top of an index finger. "What? I'm just saying…"

"Iris, you shouldn't sit on the counter," Bluebell said as she wandered back to the sofa. "Seriously, food preparation goes on there."

"I haven't had one of your muffins in three hours, Blue," Iris responded.

"Yeah, but *breathing* gives you gas."

"It's true." Hyacinth looked pointedly at Mason. "Sorry."

Primrose stared at Clover with unblinking, red-rimmed eyes. Maybe the damned things would remind her green-haired menace of a sister of the literal Hell she had suffered. Now that she finally had him warming her bed, there was no way she was letting Clover's hostility chase Mason away from it.

"Princess Preggo is back." Clover's tone was curt. "Get on with it, Prim."

Primrose looked at Mason. He nodded, silently extending permission to fill in the banks on his part of their story.

She started with how Borana, posing as Brunhilde, had enchanted Mason and ultimately sent him to Fontevraud Abbey in France to retrieve the locket. Primrose's seduction had been intentional on both their parts. Imprisoned for being a naughty nun, and terrified of being outed and burned as a witch, Primrose accepted the deal Ipos had been planning all along. At the time, none of them considered the possibility that Primrose might be Mason's potential mate.

"My one true love," Mason corrected her, wrapping his arms around her waist.

"Which is why you two found each other again," Hyacinth said, "despite all the odds being stacked against you."

"Technically, Borana had something to do with that," Primrose pointed out. "Mason would have never come looking if she hadn't left."

"Hey," Iris insisted on some of the credit, "don't forget that I had something to do with you guys finding each other, too."

Clover didn't care; she wasn't through feeling sorry for herself.

"So, Borana was just Ipos's pawn only, *now*, she's a part of my curse, too. I fall in love with her, and that makes me what, just another pawn in some ancient Mesopotamian game? I am so sick of paying for somebody else's screw-ups!"

"We all are," Hyacinth and Bluebell spoke in unison.

"Yeah!" Iris joined the bandwagon, jumping off the counter with a squeak and a thump. "It's not just you, remember? Our entire family has to live with the curse hanging over our heads."

"I know that look," Clover said, shaking her head. "You just farted, didn't you? And you're not even going to excuse yourself."

"Not to you, because you don't deserve it!" Iris flipped her a bird and looked over at Mason with doe eyes. "Excuse me, oh love of Prim's life."

"I don't think that you're just a pawn to her, Clover," Primrose went on as if the gas talk had never happened. She wished it hadn't. Why did everyone have to feel so comfortable around Mason?

"Don't go changing your story out of pity for your pathetic, emotional leper of a sister," Clover insisted.

"Don't you think that's a tad melodramatic?" Mason asked.

"Said the wolf who was sticking his *penis* in my potential *girlfriend* for several centuries," the green-haired Huxley responded, waving her fingers dismissively in Mason's direction, "which, for the record, is *not* making me feel any better!"

"I'm not changing my story, Clover." Primrose was ready to choke her. "We spoke with Borana when I broke her ties to Mason. She seemed relieved; she admitted she hated what Ipos had made her do, and she was happy to release him. Borana gave us her blessing, or as close to one as demons get."

"Yeah, but why did she do it in the first place?" Clover asked.

"You'll have to ask her that," Primrose said. "Just remember, all of this happened before you even met her—and she never offered us this kind of help, not when it was just Mason and me. Borana called you tonight, not anyone else, with that warning."

"It's true." Despite the possibility of getting yelled at, Mason put in his two cents worth again, "You may be the *only* reason Borana's willing to help at all. We owe you one."

Clover sighed, "No, you don't. A family takes care of its own, end of story."

"Which is great, but we need to can all that sidebar stuff for now." Bluebell stood, retrieving a duffel bag full of items she'd brought from her altar at home. She dumped its contents out on the coffee table, digging through them for dragonwort and frankincense. Burning them improved divination and psychic powers. "We know Ipos is coming, and, if we don't have a plan by the time he gets here, it's going to be bad."

"When are you going to pick a proper name for that kid, Blue?" Clover knelt down beside her sister to help. "Seriously, don't tell me we're just going to call her Baby. My niece doesn't deserve a life of torture."

"What do you mean?"

"Oh, come on," Clover insisted. "You *know* she'll get that stupid quote from Dirty Dancing every time somebody new hears her name for the first time."

"I'm not going to call my *baby* Baby." Bluebell widened her eyes, glancing over at Mason self-consciously. He was going to think she was such a whore. "I'd just like to meet her father first, somewhere outside of a dream. Or anyone else from his family in case they want a hand in picking her name."

"Okay, let's get back on track here!" Hyacinth approached the items on the table. "Iris, you have to stay over there."

"Aww."

"It's your fault," Clover said, "Farty McStink Butt."

"Slutty McSlut Cooch!" Iris shot back.

"Yep." Clover shot a bird from her seat on the floor, "but my slutty bits don't reek, now, do they?"

"Oh yeah?" Iris tried so hard to turn Clover's lemon tossing into lemonade that the end product made no sense, "Well, I'm the farting *champion* around here; don't you forget it!"

"Oh," Hyacinth giggled in spite of herself, "poor Santino."

"I don't do it when I'm around him." Iris tried to keep a straight face, but the grin broke through. "The man's *dead*— he's already been through enough."

"So is whatever crawled up your butt a couple of hours ago." Clover wrapped her arms around her stomach, doubling over with laughter.

Bluebell, who had been trying to keep a straight face, burst out into cackles along with them.

"Ladies!" Primrose's jaw quivered from holding back her laughter. For better or worse, she had missed having these maniacs around, "Can we please get back to the question of solving this issue with Ipos before Mason throws himself out of a window?"

CHAPTER 19
THE GRAN

"So an angel told you to talk to me?" Prisma Huxley brushed an imaginary speck of lint off her shoulder and picked up a jam filled flower biscuit from the tray on the table.

"Yes." Borana took a sip of the Scottish breakfast tea in her cup. She thought she hated tea, but the rich malty flavor proved delicious. "I was just as surprised as you are, considering the whole collaboration angle."

"Well," Prisma said, looking at the blooms and herbs in her glorious tea garden. A mechanical bird flung itself into deranged song, nearby. The melody was loud; it sounded like the airing of grievances. "When you're a nasty, evil witchy-poo like me, demons such as Ipos often approach you with business deals."

"And you make it a policy always to accept those deals?" Borana picked up another buttery cookie packed with strawberry sweetness in the center—counting calories was a human endeavor.

"Don't be judgy, dear. It's not becoming."

"Don't be ridiculous," Borana said. "I'm a *Succubus*. Everything about me is becoming."

"Some things more than others, I suppose." Prisma stared off into the distance with a slight twitch of her lips. "For instance, the glow of love for a particularly feisty, green-haired witch."

"No!" Borana sat up. "You leave her out of this."

"Don't fret. It's just between us nefarious girls, and I intend her no harm."

"No one knows who, or what, you made the bargain with." A disbelieving Borana cleared her throat and changed the subject.

"You sound like your cousin, now." Prisma gave her a sharp look. "In all fairness, I'd been experimenting with a strain of *Lophophora williamsii*—that's peyote, darling—to open my mind. I'm not even sure I knew the full truth of it at the time."

"It sounds like you figured it out. Why not tell me who you talked to; it doesn't change anything for you at this point, does it?"

"There's still enormous power in secrets—you'll learn that for yourself soon enough, dear."

"Why are you doing this?"

"Doing *what*? Running the Conjure Inn? It's an off-season at the moment, aside from demonic visitors, of course, but, I assure you, it is a profitable business."

"Don't play dumb with me." Borana found the feigned innocence insulting. "We both know I don't give a damn about your profits—why are you pretending to care about Clover? And why would you betray your family for Ipos?"

"I'm not pretending; I love my granddaughters. And if someone had to betray them, it might as well be me."

"If someone had to…? That isn't love; that's twisted."

"That *is* my love," Prisma laughed, "I'm told it's twisted as a funnel cloud. I keep my eyes on the girls in my special way, nonetheless. Once I realized there was a way, through my betrayal, to mitigate the damage to all of them, I took the deal."

"And conveniently got your locket back."

"A definite perk; yes."

"Why should I believe you?" Borana asked.

"Because I'm selfish. Everything I do for them puts this black heart of mine a little bit closer to redemption. Plus, this inn and I have learned all we can from one another. It's time for me to move on, which means you'll be the one running this place soon."

Borana blinked. Prisma smiled back at her; she topped off the tea and offered another flower-shaped biscuit. Borana took it—the darned things were addictive.

"I have no desire to run a bed and breakfast," Borana answered. "I'm getting my estate back, one way or another, and commanding a legion."

"War is passé—a petty game wherein the delusional overcompensate for penis envy with giant, destructive toys."

"Well," Borana said, slumping in the lavender cushions, "I don't give a shit."

"Others *do*; consider, for a moment, your little angel friend and her employers. Don't you think they'd do anything to prevent you from regaining social position or royal standing if you were capable of gathering forces in Hell?"

"I have no intention of battling Heaven; there are enough fascist factions in Hell, and Ipos is far worse than me," Borana growled the words, venting her frustration. It figured Heaven would be the one place that took her seriously.

"Mind your tone." Prisma's voice had an edge to it as she rang a bell, signaling for cleanup. "This inn's not so bad, and it would be a shame if anything nasty happened to you today as a result of my abominable temper. Especially when you have such a bright future ahead of you as my successor."

"That singing is unbearable," Borana wiped her fingers on a napkin before someone took it away. "Have you considered throttling the bird?"

"I couldn't possibly." Prisma stood. "It belonged to a Chinese Emperor I once knew. He was a lovely man—a bit stubborn, though."

"An Emperor, huh?"

She pointed toward one of the several flower-dotted trellises a few feet away. "Come and walk with me, dear."

"Walk where?" The yard ended with a small lake on the other

side. "You're not trying to drown me, are you?"

"Of course not," Prisma chuckled. "If I intended you harm, you would be dead by now. I'm not the type to fool around."

"So why bother with a Succubus?"

"You're aura is rather ambiguous. I appreciate that about you. Follow me and I'll show you wonders, girl. Starting today, with that angry bird—you can't blame it; no one likes to be discarded. And you *are* going to tell me more about my granddaughter, Clover."

"Clover?" Borana finally gave in. "She's sexy and confident—one of the most beautiful women I've ever seen. But we need to hurry, this isn't the time for chatting."

"Why not?"

"Primrose is in danger."

"Primrose? Of course, she is; she always *has* been. All Huxley women have a blind date with danger written into their destiny."

"Angelíta sent me here thinking there was some urgency in the matter of dealing with what Ipos has planned."

"That's quite an ironic name for an angel," Prisma said as she waved, indicating Borana should go first. "I'm not surprised; her kind are anxious about everything. It's all that sexual frustration, you know. As for your hurry, wasn't it Einstein who said time was irrelevant?"

"He said it was relative," Borana corrected her.

"Sorry, just testing." Prisma smiled as the two of them stepped through the trellis into an impossibly large space. There were dancing flowers, twirling condominiums, and one gigantic, annoying mechanical nightingale. "I detest stupid people."

"Really?" Borana looked around her. The condos, with their wrinkled little residents—she assumed they were magical senior citizens—and the disco-lions and samba-peas seemed polite or happily indifferent as they danced. The bird, however, glared. "Because my cousin..."

"Ipos is the king of them—and quite dangerous and torturous, although transparent; I *know* dear." Prisma was more interested in the reaction of her guest, who was seeing an alternate dimension, with rental properties, for the first time.

"That's why I spiked his tea when he initially stopped by—and why the vial in his possession is a dud. Perception is so one-sided most of the time."

"Spiked his tea with what?"

"With what he wanted, in a manner of speaking.

And, don't worry, time moves differently in here—past, present, and even the future. An entire day might only be an hour. Poe summed it up quite well: 'All that we see or seem is but a dream within a dream.' "

"If the dream is a nightmare."

"Your thinking is too finite." Prisma shook her head, guiding Borana over to the first in a set of never-ending hedgerows. She picked up the tip of a glistening, golden thread that meant the end or beginning of a maze. "This is not about suffering, but layers."

"Layers?"

"Of dimensions; of space and time, Borana. There are more worlds to what most of us will ever see around us."

"I think you mean there's more to what most of us will ever see in the world around us."

"If that's what you think, then it is time to stop thinking." The look Prisma gave her held absolute certainty. "Once you live long enough, encounter the right individuals, and pay the right kind of attention, you start to see the true nature of things. "

"Which is?"

"Various and exponential," the witch said, placing the golden thread in Borana's palm.

Borana wondered what other substances, aside from peyote, Prisma had experimented with in coming to that opinion.

"You just have to train your eyes to see it. There's nothing all that dangerous in the maze. See for yourself, and we'll talk once your errand is through."

"Is this thread like the one from the myth of the Minotaur?" While the term *errand* totally belittled her purpose, Borana recognized she was better off fishing for clues.

"It's cut from a similar spool, but, no—and don't say *myth* like that; myths are merely truths you haven't realized or seen." Prisma pulled a small container from her pocket and handed it over. "To help Primrose find her happy ending, you must give this vial to Hyacinth to drink."

Borana looked down at the rose-colored container. "This holds the other half of the love spell, doesn't it?"

"Yes. And Hyacinth is a sweet, round brunette—all curves and uncertainty at the moment; you can't miss her. The thread will guide you to her, in a town called Paradox, once the maze is through with you."

"Why would you give this to Hyacinth?"

"I'm not giving it to her, silly—*you* are."

"Why?"

"Because, between two evils, you should always pick the one you never tried before."

"Do you *ever* stop talking in riddles?"

"That's not a riddle." Prisma found it funny, for some reason. "It's Mae West—oh, and a word of warning: This maze is fractal and a bit mystic—that makes it ambiguous, but never deceptive. There are layers to everything; be sure to pay attention, and open all of your senses to your surroundings. The place won't let you go unless you do."

"I'm assuming there's no house I can move into if it turns out that I'm shitty at playing your game?"

"There is no house inside, and it isn't my game, but don't worry. I wouldn't even *consider* gifting you the Conjure Inn if you weren't capable. It's a neutral space, so we get all kinds of visitors. Whoever inherits the place, she must have an inkling of the sight to know what part of the spectrum, good or evil, she's *really* dealing with."

"You're kind of a stickler about things, aren't you?

"Not me," the witch replied, "this place. It does all the choosing. We're doing our best to convince it that you're the gal for the next round of its existence. So, whatever you do, remain honest—and *don't* be rude to the tree."

Borana took the vial. She crossed the threshold, trading thick, emerald grass for a pathway. Sunshine bombarded her, and the flower-dotted hedges spun in squares. It might have been her that spun; it was hard to tell because nothing had moved yet everything did all at once. Her vision felt wrong; she saw more colors, places, and things than anyone in their right mind should.

Had Prisma drugged the cookies?

Once the dizziness dwindled enough for her to focus, Borana turned toward the entrance. Just as she suspected, the way she came in was now nothing more than a solid hedge. It was also a dirty brick wall at the end of some alley. *Odd.* Regardless, there was no choice left but to move forward.

CHAPTER 20
THE ENTRANCE

"Well, even I wouldn't have guessed that," Ipos said as he turned off the engine of the twice-stolen taxicab.

The lion-headed demon smoothed back strands of his mane from his face. He ordered the battle-marked mage in the passenger seat to retrieve four big ugly coats from the trunk. None belonged to him. Ipos had decided it would be un-princely, giving his finery away to the Grays, even for safe passage. He had borrowed a plaid monstrosity instead, from one of the seven henchmen he hired for the day.

Ipos pulled a small packet of dried oatmeal from the glove compartment, along with several handfuls of iron nails and the vial. While he didn't know whether or not there was much truth to the bit about fairies and oatmeal, it couldn't hurt to test out the old wives' tale. As for the nails, he remained confident that the Sidhe—Seelie, Unseelie, and everything in between—disliked iron and steel as much as wolves did silver.

The mage, two demons from the back seat, and three more from a second cab walked with him into the small park bundled between residential neighborhoods. Prisma had warned him that all deceptions vanished upon crossing fairy barriers, so none of them wasted their energy on a disguise.

Who gave a shit if some five-year-old human spawn accidentally spotted a gang of demonic thugs crossing the road? Its parents would, no doubt, chalk that up to a vivid imagination, maybe a little brainwashing from too many violent cartoons. They might order the unpleasant little thing to lay off the sugar for a few days. Whoop-tee-do.

"Is that..." one of the red-skinned demons asked, placing a few nails into each of his pockets.

"Yes," Ipos strode to the small, roof-capped structure; it looked a bit like a mushroom. As predicted, wild thyme and morning glories surrounded the base.

"What good does a shitter without a door do?" a second one cocked his head, looking at the crescent moon carved into it.

"It's unconventional enough be a sign," the mage answered absentmindedly, stroking the outline of a crack in his face. The interior pulsed with a butt-load of stolen magic.

Nothing protruded from the sides of the wooden privy. Ipos walked clockwise around the back of the striped contraption for a look. Sure enough, there it was in the back: a shelf with the image of a nightingale above it.

"What now, boss?" A two-headed demon wearing expensive sneakers posed the question.

"Follow a few seconds behind me and do the same thing I did."

All six—four of them were worthless but exceedingly loyal for what compensation they were receiving—paid close attention as Ipos laid his borrowed coat carefully in the middle of the rack. He walked in circles, counter-clockwise, around the perimeter of the outhouse three times before vanishing along with the ugly outerwear.

There was a rush of air and a sound like breaking glass as Ipos breached the barrier on the other side. His feet landed on a path, surrounded by mushrooms, next to signage that read "Crossroads To Paradox. Population: Undeterminable." He sprinkled dried oatmeal on the animated fungi; they gobbled it up and asked for more. A few seconds later, the mage appeared, and then the third member of their party, followed by the fourth and the fifth.

Number six complained that his arms tingled. After that, there was a flash of light and the seventh, and final, demon popped into the dimension. He looked over at the others, opened his mouth to comment, and promptly burst into flames.

"Well, they know we're here," Ipos remarked, undoing the shiny buttons of his brown waistcoat as ashes and bone fell to the ground.

An obnoxious cross between the sounds of bagpipes and a cat with its tail stuck in a blender rent the air in the woods around them.

"Now!" Ipos savored the rush of adrenaline from the alarm. "Let's see what kind of Sidhe beast they send for us."

"No one cares, you know," the red-skinned henchman standing to Ipos's left snarled. He was a bit testy from the lack of warning about the possibility of spontaneous combustion via fairy magic. Spontaneous combustion, as it turned out, was a *big* deal.

"No one cares about what?" Ipos raised a sandy eyebrow halfway to his horns.

"About *you* and the length of your mane, or your shoes, or your *damned, fancy overcoats!*" He noticed the others cringing at his tone but just couldn't hold it in.

"It's a fancy waistcoat, not an overcoat. You don't know the difference because you're too pedestrian for fashion sense—and jealous of me."

"*No one* is jealous of you! Half of Hell makes fun of you behind your back."

"Only half?"

"The other half does it to your face. You're too busy admiring your reflection to notice."

"You sound just like my whore of a cousin." Ipos flexed his claws and licked at a front incisor. "I've half a mind to gut you for smarting off to me like that."

"Then you'd only have six of us left to help you face the hideous *she*-beast."

"Six is more than e..." Ipos frowned. "What did you just say?"

"The same thing you did."

"NO, it sounded like you said *she*, not Sidhe. *She* as in a woman."

"Did I?" the demon replied tartly.

"*Yes.*"

The henchman snorted. "Look, everybody knows you're a misogynist! Why wouldn't they send a *she* to kick your ass inside out and sideways in Fairy Town? It's called irony, Your Highness."

The misogyny became a moot point as the ground shook beneath their feet. Treetops rustled in the distance, scattering leaves onto the ground everywhere.

Something colossal was approaching. There were two things, actually—ogres, from the looks of them.

"Fee Fi Fo..." the younger one, a male with huge muscles, angry eyes, and a great bulbous nose roared.

"Reamann Eugene Grimm!" The gray-haired matriarch, who was enjoying being normal size again immensely, boomed at his side. "Don't you dare say fun; how many times have I warned you about puns in battle? Your father would be horrified if he could hear you!"

"Gods *dammit*, grandma! They wouldn't have known the difference!"

The magic man sent a barrage of silver nails flying in their direction; the majority struck the young one, eliciting screams of pain.

"Good to see something works as advertised," Ipos said.

The looks several of the henchmen gave him were pathetic—looks that clearly said demons had no idea what to do with ogres. Ipos calmly recommended that they figure it out and hold their ground because that was the only way anyone was getting paid.

"Don't let them chase you away from the path; you may never find it again!" the mage shouted at Ipos over the huffing and thumping of several tons of ugly now barreling down on them.

"So help me, *Lucifer*," the fashion-deficient henchman said, "if I get out of this alive, I am finding an honest job, and I'm never answering another one of your calls again."

Ipos shrugged; no great loss there. He was, however, a bit disappointed in *Prisma* for not mentioning the possibility of ogres. What was the best plan of attack here? Spinal cord? Achilles heel? Improve their hygiene? Judging by the way they stank, they were apt to be offended to no end by good hygiene.

"I'm not unskilled, you know." The idiot kept going. "I once possessed a guy who was majoring in psychology for a year."

Ipos turned to him, blatant disbelief written all over his face. *Why was he still rambling at a time like this?*

"Are you proposing we psychoanalyze these behemoths to death?"

"No, but..." Whatever he was about to say was rendered immaterial. The ogre that hated his middle name nailed the whiner in the center of his chest with one gigantic foot. The demon went flying a good three car lengths back along the path, landing on a patch of cheery mushrooms.

All that cheer went right down the crapper the moment the demon fell on them. One of the fungi bit him with its vicious little teeth. He rolled away, shrieking. Demon number three dashed out of the way to avoiding getting stomped to a pulp by ogre feet; the whiner wasn't so lucky.

Ipos dropped down on all fours to dodge an age-spotted mountain of jiggling flesh and gray hair. He circled behind the ogre and leaped, snapping and snarling and enjoying the violence.

On his first attempt, his claws hooked the back of her legs. Ipos tried charging up the ogre's huge dimpled haunches to reach a more vulnerable spot—the vertebrae, spinal cord, or throat—but failed.

Mrs. Grimm threw him off with a good deal of flailing and spinning. Her fist swung around, smacking the side of Ipos's head. The punch rocked him so badly that it took a moment to register the source of the horrible shriek that came next. It was the other ogre, Reamann. The mage sucked energy from the ground and trees surrounding them, preparing to take care of her.

The elder Grimm's priorities shifted once the yelling started, and the Sidhe-beast thudded away in the direction of her wounded grandson. Between the nails and two demons, Reamann fared poorly, bleeding profusely far from the path.

Ipos told the mage to stand down and conserve his power. Dead henchmen meant less of a payout; he could live with that. He commanded the two-headed demon—the only other companion on this venture whose life had value to him—to abandon the fight and follow him into town.

Keeping a four-legged stance for speed, Ipos dashed in the direction of the sign, down the long road to Paradox. The two-headed demon grew, sprouting wings and picking up the mage, who was not particularly happy about this, by his armpits in the interest of time.

The mushrooms put on a Biblical show, gnashing tiny teeth together and weeping. They wept for the Grimms, for the shitty coats that had been traded for passage into Paradox, and for the demonic asshole that was coming for one of Paradox's own.

CHAPTER 21
THE COMPROMISE

"What do you mean by magical Krav Maga?" Iris made a big deal out of raising her voice to ask the question.

"Well," Bluebell responded, attempting to offer a sensible enough explanation, "Krav Maga is a martial arts buffet. All sorts of disciplines are involved."

"Uh-huh," Iris egged her on, glancing over at Hyacinth. "Go ahead."

"If Ipos has talked with Gran, and he didn't happen to know our capabilities *before* then, we have to assume that she educated him."

"No, we don't," Clover interrupted. "Gran's not a hundred percent evil, you guys; at least, she wasn't the last time I ran into her. She wanted to know how we were doing."

"Will you stop with the Gran-Gran love fest?" Iris groaned at her. "I keep telling you, she's a wicked, old bitch, way worse than you are; get over it and move on like the rest of us."

"She raised us after Mom went mad!"

"She's the one who made Mom *crazy!*"

"You ran into her, and you didn't say anything?" Primrose raised her eyebrows. "First, Iris and Mason; now, you and Gran. What the hell is wrong with this family?"

"Not fair, Prim," Iris defended herself. "The thing with Mason was entirely different."

"Hey!" Bluebell screamed at them. "Limited time before the bogey lion gets here, remember? Shut up and listen! I've been pouring through an old grimoire Mason found for me downstairs; I think I can come up with a spell to borrow—or lend—powers temporarily. Just for a day or two; it should be like flipping a switch on and off."

"Sweet!" Iris said.

"Wait a minute; borrow powers from whom?" Primrose threw her hands up in agitation. Sparks of energy arced from her fingertips to the ceiling, and her hair stood on end; she looked like the electrode in a novelty plasma lamp. "Do you even know where that spell book came from? I'm not letting what I've got spread into anyone else, Blue. That's the whole reason I refused the mating bond."

"Relax," Bluebell's voice was gentle but firm, just the way she imagined a mother should be. "I wasn't thinking of you. And I don't need to know where the book came from—the store provided it when it was needed; just like Mason said it did for Mrs. Grimm on the day that he showed up here."

"This place is in the heart of Paradox, Bluebell; it's a hotbed of wild fairy magic, and it's unpredictable."

Bluebell rubbed her belly with a smile. "So are we."

Hyacinth looked a little worried. "I don't have a problem with Iris and Clover sharing their powers if they want. But I can't take yours, Blue, that leaves you defenseless."

"That's the whole point of my finding the spell, Cyn. Iris and Clover don't *need* it. You're the one who can't access your own powers, and I have no intention of battling anything other than my bladder. My pregnant ass is staying here."

"Prim, come on, you can't let her do this," Hyacinth said, looking at her eldest sister for backup. "It's wrong."

"You'll leave me out of this sharing business, right?" Primrose touched Blue's shoulder, making eye contact. Unpredictable or not, what she was going to do for Hyacinth made sense.

"Promise. As a matter of fact, why don't you go downstairs and spend some time with Mason while we work this out? I'm sure you two could use it."

"So am I." Primrose headed for the door and down the wooden steps without a second glance at anyone. If Hyacinth insisted on fighting alongside her sisters, she would just have to feel guilty about borrowing from Blue. Guilty was better than powerless.

Downstairs, Primrose walked to the front desk. She found the sprite—the one hired with the assurance it was sexless and harbored no desire to hit on Mason—who pointed her in the direction of the office. "Office" was a generous term. It was bigger than a closet, had a file cabinet, a desk and chair, and a plaque, announcing what it wanted to be when it grew up, on the door.

"Am I interrupting anything?" Primrose stepped in with a smile. "Blue's working on some spell with the girls—she sent me away for a bit."

"Interrupting?" Mason walked over to the door, pressing the weight of her body against it and twisting the lock. He yanked the shirt she was wearing from the waistband of her jeans and began unbuttoning it. It was one of his; a bit big for her, but he loved her covered in his scent. "I can't even get started without you."

Primrose placed her glasses on the top of the file cabinet and kicked her shoes off before wiggling out of her jeans. Her bra and panties joined the other items on the floor.

"You like me this way, don't you, my big, bad, wolf?" She licked at his lips as he pinned her wrists over her head. "Completely at your mercy?"

Mason bit down on her lip. He slid one hand down to cup her breast and pinch a taut nipple, just enough to make her moan. He twisted the nub a little harder, watching her eyes turn red.

"I'm not the only one, my wicked Rose. How much time do you think they're giving us?"

"Enough for some TLC," she answered. "Of course, you're a bit overdressed for that."

"Sweetheart, we can solve that problem quickly and easily." Mason slid the hand on her breast down to the curve of one hip. The other relinquished her wrists, leaving goose bumps in its wake as it followed suit. He pulled her from the door and smacked her playfully on the ass before letting go. "As long as I get to bend you over the desk afterward."

Her hands went to his belt, tossing it to the floor as he took off his shoes. The zipper and clasp on his pants were next, and his boxers followed suit. Mason ripped his collared shirt off, placing it on the desk as Primrose scraped her nails down the hard planes of his chest and muscled abdomen.

"You're beautiful," she said, pressing her lips to his warm flesh and working her way down with slow, sweet kisses. "You have been since the day I met you."

"You're the beautiful one." He wrapped a hand in her long hair, drawing her eyes upward as she took control, sliding her tongue along the length of him, "and you're mine, Rose. Whether you accept it or not, you always will be. I love you."

"I love you, too," Primrose curtailed the rest of the conversation with the warm sleeve of her mouth.

Mason gave in, throwing his head back and leaning on the desk.

Primrose knew the wolf inside of him wanted what it always did— to bite her and establish a permanent bond. Terrified of hurting him, she refused to give in, but she'd gladly give him anything and everything else. Surely that was enough.

If she sacrificed herself *now*, at least, she could do it without regrets.

CHAPTER 22
THE MAZE

The first challenge was easy for Borana to spot thanks to a hand-painted sign that read "One Isn't Poisonous. Choose."

Next to the sign were a small apple tree with rippling brown bark and green leaves, and a tall, brown-skinned woman with long green hair. They were one and the same, for all intents and purposes, with lovely green apples hanging from their boughs.

"Hello, there," the tree said. "Aren't you lovely?"

"Right back at you," Borana replied. "I don't suppose you could make this whole ordeal a little easier, could you? I'm in kind of a hurry; there's someone about to be abducted by an asshole, and she needs my help."

"I think not!" the woman sprouted thorns in response to the question. At this point, although it was admittedly odd for her, Borana decided she liked the tree much better.

"Alrighty, then!" the Succubus cocked a curvaceous hip. She looked carefully from one apple to the next, tapping her golem-painted toes and drumming her fingernails on the golden thread. There were seven pieces of fruit in total, not a one of them any different from the others. "But they look identical. How can I pick when they're all the same?"

"That's how they grow, dear," the tree said.

"Surely you know how apples work?" The woman sounded downright venomous.

"Yes," Borana answered in her *Jesus, I cannot believe what a bitch you are* voice. She reminded herself to try and be a good girl. "I do. You can bite into them, or you can chuck them in the faces of people you dislike."

"Touché," the tree chuckled, rather enjoying itself.

Borana stood for several more minutes, mumbling to herself. She tried to determine anything—some scratch, a mark, or imperfection; better yet, a stinking X that marked the spot—that made one differ from the others.

"I could pick for you if you'd like," the woman said sweetly.

"And it would most certainly poison me."

"Smart demon!" the tree responded with enthusiasm. "Now you're getting somewhere."

Borana wasn't certain what the tree meant. As far as she was concerned, there was no apple in her hands; that was *nowhere*, not somewhere.

Did she know of anything that might correlate to the apples? Seven apples, seven dwarves—no, that didn't make sense at all. Lucky number seven? If number seven were lucky, how would she know which was number one and in what direction the counting went? It all brought her back, full circle, to the fact there were no marks on the woman, the apples, or the tree.

"Can you pick one out for me?" she asked the tree.

"Oh, no, dear," it replied nicely, "I'm afraid I can't."

"Why not?" Borana pointed at the woman within the overlapping figures. "She can."

"We cannot give away the answer, and I have no desire to see you poisoned, dear."

Borana finally caught on to the game. She spoke to the woman next, "Well, then, Ms. Helpful, I would like you to pick an apple for me."

The brown-skinned woman thought for a moment, then shrugged. "Take any one of them, you idiot. It's not like it matters."

The Succubus looked up into the sky and then around at the lovely brick wall-hedges with the slight scents of cities and magic clinging to them.

"Okay, then, I choose the tree!"

"Splendid!" The tree sounded like an over-excited toddler. It clapped its leaves together and picked up its roots, doing a little dance before tearing itself away. "It's been so long since anyone's let me take them anywhere!"

"Did I win?" Borana asked the brown-skinned woman just as she was dissolving into the hedge.

"Winning is irrelevant." The woman, left with poisonous apples hanging from her arms and hair, shrugged. It was the bitchiest shrug Borana had ever seen. "You gave the right answer; *congratulations*! Now you're stuck with Pollyanna Tree Bark. You should have eaten the fruit. In the end, it would have been less painful."

"Always the sore loser, that one." The tree shook its head and started walking.

After about thirty talkative twists and turns through the maze, Borana began to understand.

"I'm sorry to interrupt your story," she said, "but is there any way to hurry this up?"

"That all depends on *you,* but there's no need to worry. We can chat for hours in here. Didn't Prisma tell you, time passes differently outside?"

Borana sighed at the ridiculousness of her situation. She was wandering through a fractal maze in another dimension, chatting with a tree. Why? All because an angel in a bar told her to go to an evil witch, and the witch said she had to do it.

"So," the tree said, "what's your name dear? You never told me."

"Borana."

"What an *interesting* name. Mine's Con, um, ifer."

"Conifer?" Borana responded. "Like an evergreen?"

"Sure," the tree cleared its throat, "Now, why don't you tell me a little about yourself?"

"I..." She heard buzzing and paused for a moment, looking around. It was a bee on a bright yellow daisy. The insect and the flower were in the same spot as they had been around the last three corners, maybe more, yet the golden thread remained untangled. "Are we going in circles?"

"Oh, no," Conifer said. "Conversationally speaking, we've only just begun. Now, where do you come from—what are you, dear?"

Borana went for shock value, hoping it would expedite things. "I'm a demon; a Succubus—from *Hell*."

"Hell?" The tree wrapped one of its branches in the crook of her arm and patted her shoulder with another confidentially. "You don't say? Please, do go on. That sounds positively exciting! What's the weather like there this time of year? Do you have humidity?"

"Humidity?" The normally surefooted Borana stumbled a bit at the question. "We have it in parts, I suppose, but none near the castle."

"Ooh," The tree caught her and kept right on walking. "You have a castle, too, do you? Why on earth would you leave *that* and come *here*?"

"I came to speak with Prisma." Finally, they were getting to the heart of the matter. "I was told she could help me rescue the sister of the woman I love. Prisma gave me something I have to deliver to them. *Now*. It's urgent."

"Don't fret, dear," the tree responded, patting her hand this time, "it will give you wrinkles. Who was it that told you about Prisma? "

"An angel."

"My *goodness*, you do keep exciting company! But why did you leave that castle of yours? You still haven't answered the question."

Borana was growing impatient. She fought the urge to growl, remembering what Prisma had said about not being rude to the tree.

"My cousin killed my parents and seized control when I was just a girl; that's not my home anymore. I haven't had one for centuries."

"Well, you do now," Conifer practically sang, as the thread leaped from Borana's hand into the path ahead and formed a door. The tree opened it with a knob that appeared and said, "That does it, then! On your way, and we'll see you when you're through!"

It occurred to Borana as she felt the tree's branches shooing her over the threshold into Paradox that she had just passed a job interview.

CHAPTER 23
THE ALARM

"Something's wrong!" Bluebell jumped up, rubbing her belly.

"I knew you shouldn't have done the spell!" Hyacinth dropped the book with the words Bluebell had insisted she practice, rushing over to the sofa. Iris and Clover stopped their sparring on the mat in the corner as well, following behind her. "Is it the baby, Blue?

She shook head. "It's not the baby or the spell, Cyn. It's *him*; he's found a way in, and he's coming."

"Ipos?" Iris asked.

"No, you idiot," Clover answered for Bluebell, "the Easter Bunny."

"Are you sure it's not indigestion?" Hyacinth suddenly realized, standing there in the loft with her sisters and trying so hard to be brave, that she was terrified.

"Trust me; I loaned you *my* magic, not the baby's," Bluebell said. "Something has happened to the Grimms. The signs tricked Ipos into taking a long way, but he is coming, and he's got company—two others—with him.

"Well, we're not ready, so *that* sucks a big one." Iris shoved her hands in her pockets, spitting out what everyone else had been thinking. "Speaking of which, I hope they're through downstairs."

"Through?" Clover gave her a look.

"Yeah, you know." Iris had no idea where to find subtlety in a dictionary, let alone use it. She moved her pelvis back and forth, making kissy faces. "Bone storming, bruising the beef curtains, burping the wolf-worm in the witch hole..."

"Okay, we get it, you perv!" Clover was tempted to summon a gust of wind to slap Iris in the face. She opted for conserving her power with a dose of irony instead. "Do you even remember the last time you got laid by something that didn't require batteries?"

The redhead shrugged, mumbling a phrase that had "years" at the end of it.

"You should just get it over with and jump Santino," Hyacinth said, startling everyone with her frankness. "I'm sure he wouldn't mind."

Iris actually blushed; it was the weirdest thing ever.

"I wasn't kidding about the mortal enemy headed our way thing." Bluebell got them back on track again. We need to warn Prim and Mason, whether they're through or not."

The warning proved unnecessary. Prim was already at the front desk, tucking in her oversized shirt and smoothing out the tangles in her hair as she listened to a member of Paradox's Council over the phone. The desk sprite had fled and, whoever was talking, they were loud and unhappy about Ipos and his henchmen having found the town.

"Are you getting called into the principal's office for corporal punishment?" Iris asked loudly as her sister hung up the phone.

"If I make it back here," Prim answered grimly, "then, yeah, it may come to that. Reemy and Mrs. Grimm finished off the invaders that stayed at the crossroads with a little help from Riding Hood, but they're both seriously injured. We're on our own."

"The Grimms will forgive you, and so will Paradox," Mason said. "In the meantime, you've got us—and you're making it back here. We won't let that bastard win."

"Agreed," Clover responded, "and we need to head out. *Now*. We have to be as far away from this store as possible when we meet Ipos and his thugs. Otherwise, we risk exposing Blue."

"Are you sure you're coming, Cyn?" Primrose gave her sister a look threaded with regret. The last thing she had ever wanted to do was expose Hyacinth to more violence. "You don't have to, you know—you can stay here, with Bluebell."

"Strength in numbers, remember?" Hyacinth cinched the small bag of herbs at her waist closed. She clutched the book of spells Bluebell had chosen resolutely to her chest. "We all have a part to play in this, Primrose, even me. Let's go."

The five of them exited onto the street. They spread across it lengthwise, accelerating to a march as Blue locked and warded the door to Volumes & Vagaries. Iris whistled western movie style and cracked a joke about the good and the bad going to meet the ugly.

No one laughed.

"Oh come on!" Iris kicked a rock out of her way. "It wasn't *that* bad."

"How can you joke at a time like this?" Clover snapped.

"How can you not?" Iris asked her.

Mason looked over at the two of them, shaking his head. If anyone had told him he would be headed to a showdown on the edge of a fairy town with four witches a few months ago, he'd have called them insane. Then again, people did a lot of crazy things for love, and he loved Rose; this might be the worst thing, but it definitely wouldn't be the last on the relationship list.

Hyacinth laced her fingers through Prim's. She thought about all the things her sisters, Primrose especially, had done for her. Scared as she was, she was still a Huxley, and she was a part of this fight.

"Whatever you have to do today," Hyacinth said as Prim squeezed the hand holding onto hers, "whatever you let out of that box inside of you, Prim, it's *okay*. You're not a monster, and you never will be; just remember that. Hang onto it, and stay away from Ipos, alright?"

Primrose kept her eyes on the road. She hated that the sidewalks were empty. Paradox had never been this still, not until today, and it was her fault. Because of her, the Grimms were hurt, her sisters were frightened, and Ipos was here.

There were only two ways she imagined this nightmare ending, and neither one of them was any good. It would all come down to the lesser of evils. Fate was a bitch to Huxley girls—it always would be.

"I love you," Prim said, "and I'll try, Cyn. I really will, but, if it comes down to saving your lives, I'm prepared to surrender."

CHAPTER 24
THE BATTLE

Three figures met them at the edge of town: Ipos, a two-headed demon with bat wings, and a big man with a deep facial crack, dressed in leather armor. Light shone through the gap in his skin; it pulsed and writhed with every heartbeat.

"How heartwarming!" Ipos remained unconcerned with Team Hell's lesser numbers. "I see you've brought your bridal party here to greet us, Primrose—and your *dog*. Sorry, but he can't come with you. I have a strict no pets rule in my household."

Mason growled, fur and claws popping out his hands as he lunged for Ipos. The man with the fractured face appeared bored. He swiped a hand to the left and uttered one word, *prestanat* (stop), in response.

A single word—that was all it took to send Mason's body flying sideways. It slammed into a second story wall at full speed. He landed with a thud, lying still.

"What in the holy hell was that?" Iris's eyes widened as Primrose rushed to Mason's side.

"Macedonian." Ipos was more than happy to elaborate. "My friend 'L' here was once employed by Alexander the Great. He even had a role in that whole conquer the world orgy during the days when Mesopotamia fell. Sadly, he and King Alex had a falling out—something about fraternizing with demons."

"And *bat boy* over there?" Clover pointed at the winged guy in the Armageddon t-shirt. He was the biggest of the bunch, a lunkhead whose muscles had muscles, and egos of their own in need of a reality check. She was so calling dibs.

"Bat boy goes by Cyril," the lion-headed demon replied cheerfully, "and he's prepared to rip your arms off and eat them at the slightest notice."

"Hyacinth," Ipos addressed the shapely brunette with a nod. "Thanks again for the directions. I assume you've figured out there is no Danny Chung by now."

"Yes." Hyacinth looked him in the eyes, a spark of anger at the betrayal lighting her own. "And I'm sorry I gave you my pen."

Ipos, genuinely nonplussed by her actions, frowned. "I'd have taken it regardless."

"I *know*," Hyacinth answered. "Because that's just the kind of monster you are."

"Pilfered pens are the least of my offenses, school teacher."

"I told you I'm not a school teacher."

"*Au contraire*. Who else brings a book to a fight?"

"I'm sure Cyn finds this reunion charming and all," Iris said, flexing her palms and igniting her fingertips, "but isn't there supposed to be more *fighting* in this battle?"

"Is there?" Ipos took note of Hyacinth's nickname. It sounded like *sin*; perhaps there was hope for the cute witch after all. "I was thinking Primrose might want to surrender and save us all the trouble of me injuring you and disemboweling her pet."

"Come on!" Clover summoned a small whirlwind between her palms, looking pointedly at Cyril. "These nice Grays cleared the streets for us; it would be a shame not to give them a show … Prim?"

Primrose moved her hand from Mason's chest and looked up at the sound of her name. Her eyes were blood red with smoldering rage.

"Yes, Prim. What's it going to be?" Ipos pulled the vial from his coat pocket. "Come here and have a little drinkie-pooh with your incredibly handsome suitor, or watch your entire family suffer?"

"You're not hurting *anyone*." Primrose hardly recognized the sound of her voice. The ground shuddered in response to each syllable; row after row of street lamps flickered on and exploded in a show of magic and glass for at least a mile behind her.

"Of course not," Ipos said, looking at the mage, "all you have to do is surrender."

"Not going to happen, jackass," Iris answered for her.

"Never mind your sister's lack of manners." Ipos glared at Iris. "I'm still standing, and so is the question. What's your answer, Primrose?"

Hyacinth moved to Mason's side, making eye contact with Prim. Sprinkling the herbs from her pouch in a circle, she opened the book and started chanting. The words were part of a protection spell, one strong enough for two—Blue had intended that Hyacinth use it on herself and Prim, if necessary.

To free her sister from her worries enough to fight, Hyacinth had to remove the distraction of worrying about Mason. There was no other way.

"I've got him; he'll be okay," she told Primrose, "and so will you. *Go.* Take care of this."

Primrose nodded and leaped to her feet, charging forward in a unified front with Clover and Iris. They didn't get far. The crack on the mage's face turned blue, pulsing and writhing, as he threw his hands up and yelled, freezing them mid-run.

"Oh, darling," Ipos was smug as he looked into her glowing eyes "Did you honestly think I'd come without the means to contro..."

Primrose remembered the sound of that voice all too well. She thought of all the things the bastard had done to her and the things he would do to her family. Prim allowed the rage that boiled inside of her to surface and ignite. She concentrated on focusing the full blast of energy into the hands of the stranger at Ipos's side.

The index finger of the mage's right hand twisted, the bone compacting. His thumb followed suit, then the middle finger. The air sang with a chain reaction of grunts and cracks. L held onto his control for several seconds while his face contorted into a mask of pain. The effort eventually became too great; he was forced to release the witches, pulling all the energy he could back into himself to heal the damage.

The two-headed demon rose higher in the air; his sneakered feet bobbed with each flap of his wings. Clover threw a sideways funnel of air at him. It spun his body in the same direction as he dove for her. She darted out of the way, and he crashed headfirst into the road beside her. The eyes looking up at her were groggy.

Clover smacked the back of one of her boots on the pavement. A sequence of gears in her heel whirred to life, triggering the toe blade. Technically, it was illegal—at least in the human realm—which always made her feel like a badass. She kicked hard, aiming right at Cyril's heart. The footwear had been a gift from a psychotic ex-girlfriend. The woman had turned out to be a barroom brawler with steampunk tendencies, but her shoemaking skills were *incredible*.

Iris darted and hurled volley after volley of flames at Ipos, intent on buying Prim time to deal with the mage. Plus, the demonic pussycat was pompous and prissy, which made her *really* want to give him split ends. The edges of his mane lit on fire—he laughed at her as if it were nothing, shaking them off. She aimed for his waistcoat next, happy to find it wasn't quite so flame retardant.

"Not so funny now, am I?" Iris dodged to get out of the way, tossing more fireballs his way as the bastard cursed and struggled to get out of his coat.

The mage held his hand, flexing each finger after reshaping it. He looked at Primrose with cold eyes as she approached. The ground beneath both of their feet cracked with the force of her intentions. He released his restored hand, flinging both arms up and began chanting, drawing her power into him.

As Primrose fought against the siphon, L's chant took on a new determination. It became one word, over and over—*son*. The light through the crack in his face slowly changed until it matched the red of her eyes.

In the back of Prim's angry haze, as she fought to keep the energy from being leeched away from her, something recognized that word. The meaning was *sleep*, and it wasn't part of any battle. It was a command, one that every fiber of her being felt compelled to obey.

"No!" she shouted, but it was already too late.

Everything inside of Prim shut down, sending her useless body tumbling to the ground.

CHAPTER 25
THE CAVALRY

The winged demon, Cyril, took to the air as Primrose collapsed. Hovering where Clover couldn't reach him, he clutched at a deep gash underneath his ripped shirt. Mildly acidic blood—a perk of the magic the paranoid Ipos had used to make him mage-proof—dripped down around his fingers, leaving marks where it fell to the road. He remained there, watching his boss approach the fallen witch.

Clover grimaced as a dot from the suspended demon splashed onto her forearm. She wiped the blood off with the hem of her shirt; better a hole in the cotton than in *her*. She had to hand it to him; Cyril's reflexes were quick. Her first kick had missed him altogether. The next one hit home, albeit several inches off base.

There was a dull ache in the back of Clover's thigh—one that, annoyingly enough, involved part of one buttock. She might have pulled a hamstring. *Awesome.* Another sign she'd been avoiding the gym for too long. Her eyes followed Cyril's over to her oldest sister, a feeling of dread sinking in.

"Enough!" Ipos shouted, rolling his eyes at Iris. She kept hurling fireballs, even as he stalked over to Primrose. The thick silver rings on his fingers—ones he had intended to assault Mason with—still glowed from the heat of her fire. "You already owe me a jacket, witch; don't tempt me! If you damage my prize, I might have to replace it with your skin."

"Now," Ipos said as he knelt next to his bride to be. He ran a handful of fingers over her cheek while Hyacinth and the others watched in horror, "I've had enough of the hiding and games, Primrose. I know you can hear me in there, and, I must tell you, my friend here knows lots about containment and control. From now on, the three of us—you, me, and L— are going to be inseparable."

While Ipos spoke, a gold door appeared beside Mason's unconscious form. Borana quietly tumbled through it, inside of the protection spell. She tripped over Mason, catching a toe on his ribs, and fell straight into the voluptuous, brown-haired Hyacinth.

"Oh, good!"

Hyacinth dropped the spell book—it banged and echoed loudly around the three of them—and caught her. Several of Conifer's leaves still clung to Borana's shoulders. She looked down at Mason. Then she looked around, assessing the situation.

Borana recognized the mage. She could now see the man was a hollow shell stuffed with stolen power—like a porcelain doll with no innards to call its own. Primrose was down, and Ipos was large and in charge, just as he had planned. She shoved the vial into Hyacinth's hand with no further ado.

"Here," she said, "you have to drink this."

"Who *are* you?" Understandably, Hyacinth didn't exactly trust this sudden, demonic newcomer in a tight dress. Or the tiny bottle with the words "drink to activate" scrawled on its side, "And what is that?"

"I'm Borana: your sister may have mentioned me," she answered while Ipos made a Shakespearean production out of Primrose's condition and his plans for the rest of her immortal life, "and that thing in your hand is a love potion."

"What's he got, then?" Hyacinth pointed the vial at the matching one in the blowhard's hand. It seemed odd that no one had noticed Borana's spectacular arrival. Not even Clover. Admittedly, there was a crisis in full swing—but how often did demons and doors just appear out of nowhere?

"Ipos has a dud. Look, we have a limited window of opportunity here. Your grandmother Prisma sent me; she says the only way to give Primrose and Mason their happy ending is for you to drink this. Post haste."

"I don't trust my grandmother—or you." She had never heard Gran use the phrase *post haste*.

"I don't blame you," Borana replied, "family ties and all, but you might want to on this one. The guy with the glowing crack in his face has some serious firepower. I'm talking legendary in the demonic community. Ipos is going to take your sister. Primrose will spend the rest of her immortal life shackled and miserable in Hell unless you drink the other half of the potion."

"The other half?" Hyacinth looked at the lion-headed demon, processing the information. She jabbed a finger at the air and watched it ripple, confirming her suspicion that the protection spell had become a full-blown privacy shield. The world outside was now moving in slow motion thanks to the fairy magic piggybacking off the protection spell.

"*Yes*, the other half." Borana felt sorry for Hyacinth, but she also recognized that what Prisma had planned was better than the alternative. "The Lion Schlemiel over there, he thinks the whole deal is one-sided, but it isn't. Prisma snuck part one down his gullet the day he approached her to set the wheels for this whole fiasco in motion."

"So, let me make sure I have this straight." Hyacinth frowned, "I drink this, he falls in love with me, and vice versa? My grandmother wants this to happen?"

"Look, if it helps any, I think she's taken a page from Sun Tzu's book: The most brilliant general is the one that wins without fighting."

"That's the guy that wrote The Art of War, right?" Hyacinth looked at Mason as he stirred by Borana's feet. Paradox's magic *did* appear to be doing its part to slow down the events outside of their bubble—and to keep the Succubus concealed. There had to be a reason for that: Borana's intentions were decent. She genuinely was helping the town protect one of its own.

Hyacinth twisted open the vial. "For the record, I'm not big on the vice versa; is there a way to undo the love, afterward?"

Borana sighed as disgusting sprinkles of effervescent emotion floated out of the bottle to greet them. The potion was incredibly cheery; the only things missing were confetti and fanfare.

"Prisma didn't mention any. If it helps, please know I intend to explain to your sisters. Surely they can do some witch forensics to figure out how to reverse it."

"Please do." Hyacinth nodded, placing the legitimate vial to her lips. She drank as Ipos poured the contents of the dud container down Prim's throat. The thin liquid tickled her palate and coated her esophagus with love sonnets and liquid sunshine. Something told her that, if she knew any better, she would hate herself after this. "Loving Ipos is wrong on so many levels. Being stuck with another asshole for the rest of my life is so not my idea of fulfillment."

"I understand." Borana meant it. "Seriously, I wouldn't wish him on my worst enemy, and he *is* my worst enemy."

"Borana?" Mason rolled to his side, staring at the two of them. His foot tapped the edge of the invisible shield as he got his bearings. "What's going on?"

"Hello, Fur Ball. Nice of you to join us," Borana said. "You want to know what's going on? Primrose is asleep, Ipos is in control, and Hyacinth just drank a love potion."

"She did what?" Mason climbed to his feet.

"Don't look at me like that," Borana said. "It's not as if you were any help to them lying there, unconscious on the ground."

Mason opened his mouth for a rebuttal, but the door reappeared. Several pairs of branches hauled the Succubus away before he could think of anything to say.

"I'll be in touch!" Borana yelled at him. She sincerely wished she could have blown up something—*anything*—like they did in the movies. "Mason, make sure you save the vial for witch forensics!"

CHAPTER 26

THE LOVE

"You shouldn't have done it," Mason placed a hand on Hyacinth's shoulder as the invisible fairy curtain fell away from the two of them.

"I had no choice," Hyacinth answered. There was an odd tingling in her stomach; she assumed it was Prisma's strange brew going to work. "Gran set this all in motion to save Prim. Maybe it won't be that bad; he has no choice but to love me in return."

"Ipos is a monster, and you don't deserve this. It's like saying no good deed is going unpunished."

"Get used to it; Gran's twisted that way," Hyacinth said as she slid the vial into Mason's palm. "Would you mind hanging on to this for me? I'm starting to feel funny, and I don't think it's a good idea for me to…"

"Take your paws off her!" Ipos roared when he looked up and saw them. The demon leaped to his feet, with his lightly singed mane bristling and his claws extended.

Clover and Iris glanced at one another and then at Prim's body while Ipos stormed off in Hyacinth's direction.

"Mason's with Cyn," Clover said. "We need to get Prim out of here, first. You grab her legs; I'll get her head."

They attempted to do just that. The mage, who was offended by them acting as if he, the most magically powerful of them all, wasn't even there, allowed them to come within inches. Then he shook his head, flicked his fingers, and said *ladno*, which meant cold, freezing the pair in place.

"Now *this* is just a big old pile of icy bullshit!" Iris rolled her eyes to the side, peering at Clover.

"Oh, good!" Clover peered back at her, disgusted. "At least you can still complain."

The crack-faced mage remained stoic, but Cyril laughed from somewhere behind them. The sound of his leathery wings slapping the air, along with the occasional hiss of acid dripping on the pavement, grew closer. Apparently, Iris had won herself a fan.

"Yeah, well, somebody ought to; have you looked at that *face*?" she complained. "It's like Ipos opened a big old can of ugly. I bet every time this asshole looks in the mirror, his reflection has to look away."

Cyril snorted, and L glared—Clover started to realize (oh, happy day) that maybe Iris might be on to something. Despite the fact he hadn't spoken it in front of them, the Macedonian understood English just fine. Bonus: His looks were a sore spot, and Cyril was looking for some amusement. Good thing Iris Huxley was the queen of insults.

"They had to put tinted windows in his incubator!"

Cyril slapped his thigh beside them, his shoulders shaking with laughter.

"He couldn't get a date off a calendar!"

The mage took his eyes off the witches, full on glaring at the winged demon. Cyril hooted and bounced in the air, wiping tears from his eyes. "Oh, man, L, she's got your number!"

"Good girl," Clover muttered, wiggling her fingers and toes, "you're breaking his concentration. Don't stop now; go for the jugular."

"He can't cut onions because he makes *them* cry!"

The light from the crack in the mage's face dimmed.

Iris hurled more insults, egging on Cyril's laughter until L finally leaped for the demon's throat. He might not have made it, if not for Clover boosting him with a heavy-handed shot of wind.

Free of the cold, Iris and Clover rushed to Prim and dropped to their knees. They called her name, shook her shoulders, and even tried slapping her; the two tried anything and everything they could think of in their attempts to wake their sister. Meanwhile, Ipos stood outside the protection spell roaring at Mason, also to no avail.

"Come out here so I can string your intestines up on the street lamps, you flea-ridden coward!"

Mason growled, more than happy to give the evil jerk a fight, but Hyacinth gripped his shirt, holding him back.

"No," she said, glaring at Ipos.

"Why?" Ipos was adamant.

"Because Prim loves him, and you are a psychopath who would disembowel him."

"Of course, I would." Ipos didn't bother denying it. "He touched you!"

"So?" She flattened her palm against Mason's chest. "Look, I'm touching him *back* now. We're even; it's fine!"

"Stop that! He's a mangy dog, and you are a queen. Mason doesn't deserve to lick the shit from your heels."

"Wow," Mason mumbled. "That stuff *really* worked, didn't it?"

"I'm not wearing heels or..." Hyacinth said, scrunching up her face—she just couldn't bring herself to repeat the word, "*that* on my feet!"

"You can't even say 'shit' can you?" Ipos shook his head with an infatuated smile. "That is so adorable."

"Hyacinth," Mason couldn't take the two of them anymore, "you need to let me go to Rose before I throw up all over the two of you."

"Yes, by all means, let the puppy go," Ipos agreed as a whirlwind of demon wings and mage power tumbled over all of their heads, crashing into the Council's Main Hall. "Let him go, and come with me."

"Only if you do the same with Primrose." Hyacinth grew bolder and Mason stilled, waiting for the answer.

"That's different; I *need* her."

"It's no different."

"Hyacinth," Ipos frowned, "you don't understand. I worked so hard—all the plotting, and torturing, and subterfuge to get her."

Hyacinth recognized that sound in Ipos's voice; it was pleading. Preston had never begged for *anything*. He made her do all the sobbing, and beseeching, and entreating. He had bullied and taken, breaking her down like a collapsible child's toy. Now, for once in her life, true love or not, she realized that the power was in her hands.

It was a marvelous feeling.

"Don't tell *me* I don't understand. Believe me; I know perfectly well." She straightened her spine and stood her ground. "It is not different. You can either have Primrose or have me—but you will *never* have both of us."

"But," Ipos protested, "her *power...*"

"Won't make you happy," Hyacinth answered, releasing Mason so that he could go to Primrose. "You can beat her, lock her up, and keep her away from all that she loves. You can break her repeatedly, but neither one of you will ever find your happiness. I'm certain of it; I have lived the other end of that life, Ipos."

There was a long pause—one that, admittedly, involved a few calculations on Ipos's part. Hyacinth was exquisite; he felt an attraction to her earlier, long before this whole potion business. While he could probably do without ever having love in his life again—all that tenderness tugging at his heartstrings had been downright bothersome—she was a Huxley.

"I see," he said.

Not only was she a Huxley, but she was also *the* Huxley—the one that Prisma, that sly old witch, had wanted him to take home all along. Why shouldn't he enjoy naked time with the fairest of them all? Hyacinth could still give him access to Primrose as an in-law, and he *would* eventually win the family's trust. In the meantime, he could finally dress that beautiful body up in the finery that it deserved and give it lots and lots of well-deserved attention.

"Without question, I choose you, Hyacinth. On one condition: You must come home with me to Hell, *immediately*—no stalling, no running, and no hiding. We have a wedding to plan."

"Prim and Mason's? I don't think so; they wouldn't like that at all."

"Not Prim and Mason's," Ipos responded, "I couldn't care less about their nuptials. We are planning *ours*."

"Isn't that a bit sudden?" Hyacinth was sure that it was. Loving a monster in a cravat was one thing, but being trapped in marriage with him, right away, based on emotions that came from a bottle? No, thank you. "I agree to come back with you, but I think we should live together."

"For a few weeks."

"Six months."

"One month." Ipos's counteroffer was determined.

"You have an abominable need to control everything, don't you?"

Maybe she could talk herself out of the attraction, eventually. So what if there was a muscular chest and tight pants with bulging thighs beneath the arrogant lion-head? So what if he had plump, kissable lips, and a luxurious mane? He was still a bad pers—um, demon.

"An abominable need? Don't be ridiculous," he said. "I'm giving up ultimate power for you, my love."

"Other than Primrose."

"*Other* than her? Well, yes," the demon answered, "I suppose I do like to control everything. It's a character flaw—something you can work on improving."

"*Three* months and I get to say goodbye." Hyacinth looked to the spot where her sister still lay fast asleep. Mason, Iris, and Clover knelt around her. "If the candlesticks sing or the wardrobe smacks me, I'm coming back. Immediately."

"Three months," he agreed, unperturbed by the fact she was mocking him. Anyone else might have suffered for the insolence; on her, it was adorable.

"What about the mage's spell?"

"I have no idea how to break it." Ipos shrugged, looking over Hyacinth's shoulder at the fight between demon and mage. It was still going strong.

"L prefers more fear than ridicule from his opponents," he said, "and he's a bit *sensitive* about his complexion. There's no way he will help, not after the way those two insulted him. Your sisters will just have to find another way."

CHAPTER 27
THE AWKWARD

"Cease this idiocy at once!" Ipos commanded the magic man and Cyril. Both were now taking swings at each other, old-fashioned fisticuffs style, in the street.

The two-headed demon had been doing quite well, with the mage taking twice the number of hits in their skirmish. L was more concerned about moving his face out of range than he was with fighting an impudent, t-shirted demon immune to his siphoned magic. He couldn't afford any more cracks—the jokes were bad enough already.

The two of them paused. They looked to the Prince whose burned coattails they were hitching a ride on expectantly, then to Hyacinth with more than a little curiosity.

"This is witch trickery," the mage said. "She is not the one you need, Ipos! There is nothing of value inside of this one."

"Harsh much?" Cyril elbowed him in the ribs, realizing the other members of the family were staring back at the scene. The winged demon was starting to understand the appeal of Huxley witches—particularly when it came to one sharp-mouthed, funny redhead.

"You're wrong," Ipos answered. "Her value is inestimable to me— and to *you* if you wish to receive any form of compensation."

Iris moved her hand from Prim's, climbing to her feet with a frown. "Mason, do you have any idea what's going on over there?"

"Fallout from a love spell," he answered grimly.

"Is that what he poured down Prim's throat?" Clover stood up, too. "You've got three seconds to start talking, or I'm blowing you back into the side of another building."

Mason explained the scene he woke up to inside the protection spell. Clover was furious over the betrayal. It made no difference that Hyacinth had given consent, any hopes for forgiveness Borana might have harbored were rendered useless.

"Borana said she'd save a dance for me when this was all through," Clover said, cracking her neck, then her knuckles. "I'll dance on her face if she dares come near this family again."

"About the face dancing," Iris responded after loudly clearing her throat. "You know that still sounds like sex, right?"

Mason looked at Iris as if she'd lost her mind.

"Shut up, Sparky!" Clover shouted, the wind picking up around her as she marched over to Ipos and Hyacinth.

"I don't know what you think your deal with Cyn is, you perv," she told Ipos, not feeling the need to be polite about it, "but you keep your hands off my sister!"

Ipos raised a fuzzy eyebrow at Hyacinth before turning to Clover. He answered with the ends of his mane flapping wildly in the breeze—all except for the butchered part, "My *deal* is that she agreed to come home with me in return for my leaving Primrose alone."

"Witch trickery," L glared at her, crossing his arms in front of his chest. The light in his face had dulled even more from the exertion of fighting Cyril.

"You want to fix this, too, huh?" Clover asked.

"Duh," Cyril winked at Iris, who left Prim and Mason to come over and back up her windy sister.

"No one's undoing anything," Ipos said.

"Technically, I think Gran cou…" Hyacinth started to correct him.

"*No one*," the demon repeated himself. "I'm willing to give this love thing a shot, and so is Hyacinth."

"Yeah," Iris said, "but she's only doing that to save…"

"Let it go," Hyacinth cautioned her, squatting to pick up the book of spells.

"L can help your sister get her powers back. Not by violent means, I assure you. I wouldn't allow it." Ipos looked from Clover to Iris, his face smug. "You didn't honestly think I'd overlook an entire *witch* missing, did you? I'm assuming Bluebell hasn't given her powers to Hyacinth permanently. Although, poor dear, there must be something *terribly* wrong for her to miss out on being here."

"Nothing major—just a bad case of the witch-flu." Hyacinth handed the book to Iris and widened her eyes in warning. Ipos didn't need to hear the Super Baby news. "Please give this back to Blue, along with a big bowl of *chicken soup*, and tell her not to worry about me; I'm going to be fine."

"Any chance your porcelain princess in leather over there's willing to wake our sister up?" Clover asked as nicely as she knew how.

L curled his lip at the two sisters; he didn't bother dignifying the query with an answer.

"That's a Hell, no," Ipos responded, taking Hyacinth's hand. "You girls are on your own—and we're heading back to the crossroads. My men and I have overstayed our welcome in Paradox."

"But my sister's always welcome here," Clover told him. "Stay in touch, Cyn. We'll find a way to fix this—all of it! If that bastard hurts you or does anything you don't like, anything at all, you let us know, okay?"

"Come along, love." Tired of waiting, Ipos scooped Hyacinth up in his arms. Both sisters rolled their eyes at the caveman tactics; Hyacinth thought it was rather nice—he hadn't even grunted at her weight. "You can call them later, after settling in. We need to get started; there are only three months left for us to plan the biggest wedding Hell has ever seen."

"I'll be in touch!" Hyacinth yelled the words back over the demon's shoulder as they departed, flanked by Cyril and L. "Seriously! Don't worry!"

CHAPTER 28
THE CASKET

"Is this absolutely necessary?"

Mason pressed his hands against the smooth glass. The container was transparent, six and a half feet in length, and two feet wide. It had a cushioned interior lined with the finest ghost white silk.

"We don't want her taking up sleepwalking again; the last time she did, she blew up the only museum in Paradox." Riding Hood crossed her arms, nodding at the figure resting inside. "The Olympian exhibit, Zeus in particular, appeared to offend her. Is that what you've taken to calling her now: Rose?"

"Not just now," he said. "From the first day we met, she has always been my Rose—why?"

"It's fitting," Hood answered. "*Dornröschen*—Little Briar Rose—that's where the tale of Sleeping Beauty came from."

"But the whole glass casket thing, that's Snow White's, right?" Iris asked.

"You're too old to believe everything you see in the movies," Hood told her. "This *casket*, as you call it, has sheltered many, but belongs to none."

"Yeah," Iris said. "In case you haven't noticed, hood girl, I'm not a spiritually attuned Shaolin Monk, wandering Paradox like Carradine in a '70s TV show. You've got to break the deets down like you would for a child with Attention Deficit Disorder. I don't think I have it, but Clover swears the technique works for me."

"Deets?"

"Details, dumbass."

Mason took his eyes off the sleeping figure to glance at Iris. Her mouth was a gun with a broken trigger, shooting indiscriminately in all directions. Even Rose had said Hood was old and powerful; of course, she also had a thing for wolves. He could probably sweet talk Hood out of murdering Iris if it came to that.

"She meant that more respectfully than it sounds," Mason said. His hands were getting fingerprints all over the glass, but he didn't care. If there had been enough room, he'd have crawled in there beside Rose, no matter who told him not to.

Riding Hood winked in response, telling him she was a big girl. She'd let him know if her feelings got a booboo, and she needed him to kiss it and make it all better.

"Hey!" Iris's tone was less than cordial. "That's Prim's true love you're talking to, remember? She's right here—*sleeping,* not dead."

Mason could handle Riding Hood. Clover, who was back at Volumes & Vagaries with Bluebell, digging through books for anything she could find on Macedonian sleeping spells, was the only one that worried him.

"This container," Riding Hood explained, "is a magical suspended animation chamber. The energy required to sustain it—its price, if you will—is obtained seamlessly, at a molecular level, from its visitors and viewers."

"The Grimms got banged up pretty badly." Iris still didn't get why her sister was in there. "And the Council was furious at Prim for bringing Ipos here. You'd think they'd be happy to see her dead."

"Primrose is inherently good. She's also more powerful than you even know," Riding Hood admitted. "Sleep-walking was only one of the problems she had when she first came here."

"What's she talking about?" Mason asked Iris.

"I don't know." Iris frowned "She never said anything about it, not even to Cyn."

"Exactly," Robin Hood said with a nod. "If she wants to share with you, she can tell you after she awakens. For now, just know that Paradox intervened on her behalf today, just as you did. And I heard about the phone call. Don't be fooled; not everyone is angry. Even if the entire Council *did* have a gigantic stick up their collective ass, it has no power to deny the will of this place."

"I know Rose, Hood." Mason was still uncertain. "She spent centuries hiding; it's made her a very private person. I don't imagine she'll be happy waking up in this thing, outside, smack dab in the middle of town."

"Would you rather your borderline agoraphobic love wake up in a hospital bed with a feeding tube, a diaper, and restraints?" Riding Hood put it into perspective for him. "This is the most dignified option, Mason. No one is touching her, there will be no invasive procedures, and your Rose, along with everyone else, will remain safe."

"I never said she was crazy; she's just overly fond of her privacy," Mason sighed, looking at the long lashes resting against her pale cheeks. There was nothing he wouldn't give to see the red and hazel eyes behind those lids again. "But you're right. We'll get her through this, and then deal with it."

"Wisely spoken," Hood responded, glancing at Iris, then down at Mason's Alpha ring. "The girls have the research angle covered. I believe there is still some potential divide between our slumbering flower here and the world of wolf politics?"

"How did you know about that?" Mason frowned.

"Mrs. Grimm," Hood answered. "She and Primrose have always been close. I suggest you come clean with your pack and discuss how you wish to handle things before Primrose awakens. That is, assuming you still want to claim her as your mate? The pack could always ask you to step down; you know—or challenge you to fight for your position if you don't."

"Back off, woman," Iris answered for him. "He does."

"I do." He needed to come clean with the pack, anyway; it was the right thing to do.

It did raise questions, though. They had all been fooled by a Succubus—not just misled but deliberately poisoned and almost *killed*—due to Ipos's desire for the eldest Huxley. And Rose was responsible for Preston's death.

Preston's sister, Lela, was a part of his pack, now. Would they understand that none of it was Rose's fault?

If not, would they ever be able to forgive Mason for claiming her, let alone accept her as their Alpha's mate?

CHAPTER 29
THE RESEARCH

"Any luck?" Iris asked, walking up to the reception desk in Volumes & Vagaries.

Officially, the store was closed; the proprietor, Primrose, slept on the street, and the people of Paradox mourned until her return from the world of dreams. Ipos and his thugs, along with Hyacinth, had fled. Bluebell and Clover had seen no need to lock the front door, especially not with Iris and Mason still outside.

"Nope," Clover said, looking up from the pile of open books sprawled in front of her. "If you ask me, this place is broken. We're looking for magic, and it keeps throwing mythology at me—no joke. It's hurling books on the subject off the shelves and into my face."

"Nothing to do with Macedonia, I take it?"

"None that I can tell—more like the Greeks."

"Isn't that pretty much the same thing as Macedonia?"

"Nope. Greece and Macedonia share a border, but their stuff's different," Clover responded, paraphrasing the title of one of the other books that had fallen on top of her. "Apparently, folks get pretty upset over modern times trying to make ancient Macedonia wear a Grecian history hat."

"That's a big stack to be flat out wrong about." Iris counted thirteen books. "If it's mythology, maybe it's trying to help Blue, instead.

Where is she?"

"Upstairs, taking a nap and avoiding the heavy paper fallout—and that's not the vibe Baby Huxley is getting. She thinks it still applies to Prim, somehow."

"Alright, then you and I will figure it out," Iris said as she slipped behind the counter alongside her sister, wondering where to start with the materials. "Mason's gone to deal with his pack. Hood thought he should come clean while we're finding a way to wake Prim, and he agreed."

Clover paused, tapping the side of a book. "I don't like it."

"You're not the Alpha to a bunch of wolves," Iris answered, "as much as you'd *like* to be, so it's not your decision to make. Hood said they could ask him to step down, challenge him if he doesn't. He still wants to come clean about everything. You've got to admire that."

"He *lied* to Prim. There's nothing good about being the one who got her into this mess."

"Don't be an asshat. Your girlfriend, Borana, was the one who pulled the strings." Iris scanned several of the book pages in front of her. "Did you open all these up by hand?"

"No, they opened to those pages when they fell," Clover answered. "And don't call that demonic liar my girlfriend; I want nothing to do with her."

"Neither did he; she was working her man-eater mojo on him, remember?"

Iris grabbed a whiteboard and supplies from a wall in the office. She figured compiling a checklist should make things easier for them. It turned out that the first generation of Titans was a recurring theme in just about all of them.

There was one mention of titanium, which they figured actually *was* an error. Titans and titanium weren't that far apart in the dictionary. Other than that, it had nothing to do with anything. The metal hadn't been discovered until 1791 by an English pastor by the last name of Gregor.

There were also three references to a place called Tartarus—one that quoted Zeus on how Tartarus was as far beneath Hades as Earth was from heaven. The subject appeared to be more pertinent since Zeus was the one who had imprisoned Titans there.

"Okay," Clover said and pointed to the twelve names on the board, "we've got six boys and six girls here. What do we know about them?"

"Boys first." Iris went down the list. "Coeus: the god of intelligence, sight and wisdom, and oracles. Crius: the god of constellations, associated with spring. Cronus: the destructive and all-devouring god of time and all the ages. Hyperion: the god of sunlight, linked to the cycles of the sun and moon, and with days and months. Iapetus: the god of life spans and death. Oceanus: originally the god of all water, but later he was bumped down to just the salty stuff."

"And the girls?" Clover asked.

"Mnemosyne: the goddess of memory and remembrance, also writing and speech. Phoebe: the goddess of brightness and radiance, a bit prophetic, did the Delphic oracle thing. Rhea: the goddess of fertility and motherhood, associated with comfort and ease. Theia: the goddess of shining light, linked to sight, metal, and jewels. Themis: the goddess of justice, morality, divine law, and order. Thetys: the goddess of rivers, streams, and all that fresh water jazz."

"We know one thing already," Clover responded.

"What?"

"That the Greek system was as sexist as ours; girl gods got the short end of the stick."

"I don't know," Iris said. "Justice is a huge deal, so Themis was okay—and Oceanus had salt water, which is lame. Nothing for him to brag about."

With a list of twelve siblings on the board and no idea what else to do with them, they took a look at Tartarus next. It was considered both a deity and a spot in the underworld, the place where the newer Greek gods sent all the old baddies. From what they could find, none of the girl Titans went, and most of the boys did. Oceanus was the exception. The watery god had no interest in power, so he didn't join the other five in the war that got them tossed down there.

"So we have five Titans imprisoned and forever condemned to Tartarus." Iris scratched her head, staring at the board. "And still no idea what they have to do with Prim."

"Well." Bluebell, who had come downstairs, walked up to the counter with one hand on her stomach. "Maybe it was one of *them*."

"What was one of them?" Clover asked.

"No one knows who Gran made her deal with—Hell's never claimed it."

"Yeah," Iris agreed, "but the gods all faded away over time. They're spirits now, nowhere near that powerful."

"You just said five were locked away in Tartarus; what if it didn't fade?" Blue asked. "Tartarus was designed as the nastiest prison ever—real old school torture. It probably made Attica and Russian Gulags look like daycare for preschoolers, right?"

Iris and Clover nodded.

"And you wrote here," Blue said it because knew Iris's sloppy handwriting anywhere, "that the place was so powerful it was considered a deity. The new gods didn't want the old ones ever to escape or forget why they were there. It was designed to be endless, eternal—*unfading*. What if Gran managed to find it?"

"Wait," Clover said. "You're honestly saying you think our Gran found a Titan prison, with *full-fledged*, pissed off gods still trapped inside, and she made a deal with one of them?"

"We've got nothing else to go on." Iris was already sold on the idea. "Hood *did* say Prim did some sleepwalking and blew up their museum. That sounds like one of them in the driver's seat, doesn't it? They had stuff on Zeus in there, and it pissed him off. Which one is he, though? We've got five left to choose from."

"Time," Clover said, looking back at the board.

"What about it?" Bluebell stared back at her.

"The dream that woke you up at 2:30; the one you shared with us. There was a timepiece, Blue—*time*."

"Iris," Bluebell asked, "who's associated with time?"

"We've got two suspects." Iris swaggered to the board, milking the sudden detective vibe as she tapped a finger at both names. "Cronus and Iapetus."

"Iapetus would be the lesser of evils," Bluebell sighed.

"Destructive and all-devouring says it all: Cronus castrated his own father."

"But our luck doesn't work that way," Iris said.

"We're in agreement, then," Clover responded. "It's Cronus."

"Hey!" Iris's attention took a sudden detour. "That Coeus guy is tied to sight and oracles. Maybe he knows the baby's..."

"One thing at a time, Ms. Attention Deficit Disorder," Clover cut her off. "First, we need to figure out what to do now that we know about Cronus."

CHAPTER 30
THE MEETING

"And that's the whole story," Mason said as he folded his hands and leaned over the conference table. He ignored the twinge in his ribs from the recent challenge to his leadership; he was more upset over wasting his best suit on this pompous ass.

The Coleman Alpha made no bones about the fact he found every last member of the Géroux pack lacking. He had shared the opinion when he met with Mason after hearing his sister was determined to marry one, and it hadn't changed. He told Mason they were nothing more than a band of outcasts, conmen, and misfits that clawed their way to a semblance of legitimacy after countless years on the fringes.

They had no "rightful pedigree."

"A mongrel's witch killed my brother," Randal Coleman growled from the opposite side of the table. "What would you want to do about it, if you found yourself in my shoes? "

Lela Coleman-Bellamy sat beside her brother. She averted her eyes, toying with her wedding band. In spite of everything, Mason still felt badly for her; she should never have asked that of her husband.

Mason had won the challenge for leadership, at the price of one broken rib and two more bruised. His accelerated shifter genes had taken care of the lesser injuries already, but the break was still healing. Lela's husband, who had been admitted to an Intensive Care Unit in a shifter-friendly hospital, found their encounter far more costly.

"What I would want to do and what I *would* do are two different things." Mason refused to be intimidated.

He was physically bigger; the bastard's shoes wouldn't fit, not that he would ever wear them. The Coleman pack was nothing but a club for old world spoon-fed elitists. Whatever it took to pound the truth through the Alpha's thick skull and into his overprivileged brain today, he was going to do it. Mason wouldn't leave until he was sure he'd stopped Randal's threats from becoming a wedge between him and Rose.

"Meaning what?" Randal challenged.

"Meaning Hyacinth was clearly being abused. Regardless of what she first saw in your little brother, and whatever face he may have shown you, Preston was a monster. He cut Rose's sister off from the outside world and tortured her relentlessly."

Lela fidgeted in her chair. Her husband's challenge had united the pack and made them stronger. The group had unanimously agreed that Mason deserved their loyalty. And Mason insisted that Lela and her mate still belonged in spite of everything that had happened. Given the same situation, most Alphas would not have been so kind.

"So you say." Randal remained curt; he was clearly not impressed. "But words aren't *proof.* You have provided nothing concrete— I have no reason to take anyone's side against Preston. All I know for certain is that some witch on a power binge killed my brother, and you are determined to align with her."

"That power," Mason defended her, "is a burden she struggles with every day. Rose is better than both of us, Randal. She has never wanted to kill anything. Preston was acting crazy. He sliced Hyacinth's throat open; the girl bears the scar as a memento."

"She was angry and seeking justice," Randal said it with a shrug, but the fury in his eyes belied disinterest. He wasn't letting anything go; the decision had been made the moment he agreed to a meeting. "Why shouldn't I do that for my own family?"

"Randal." Lela raised her head, looking at him in earnest, "He came to see me once before he disappeared."

"And?" Randal frowned. Lela had done as he asked with the challenge—why break the silence now?

"Preston wasn't himself." Lela placed a hand on her brother's shoulder as she talked, forcing him to truly look at her. "He seemed jittery—way too much energy. I think he was on something, but I didn't want to ask him about it. We had a decent visit; it wasn't worth making him angry. You know how bad he could get."

"It would make sense," Mason spoke quietly, running a hand through his hair. "Prim said he was huge; bigger than a normal wolf, and he was enraged that night."

"Do you think he was taking drugs?" Randal was done talking with Mason. "Is this something I need to have the pack look into, Lela?"

"I do," Lela answered. "I have no idea what it was or who he got it from, but it had him amped, and he wasn't a nice person to begin with."

Randal grabbed a glass and a decanter of Scotch from a tray in the center of the table while his sister spoke. The piece was Italian, made of mirror polished steel—an overpriced trinket, but Preston had been quite fond of it. He poured a healthy portion of the liquid and swirled it around before taking a sip.

"Why did Preston leave in the first place? He hadn't angered you any more than usual, and he had it good here, Randal. He was the Alpha's brother, and that made him untouchable. Mad as I was to hear how Preston died, I believe Mason is telling us the truth."

"Why?"

"I've been in the Géroux pack for several years now," she answered. "He may have attained his position in ways you disapprove of, but that's not how he maintained it. I know a good leader—a real Alpha—when I see one."

"My sister's word is good enough for me." Randal's mouth set in a grim line as he stood. He had lost Preston, and now he was in danger of losing Lela; it was time to move on. "That's as close to forgiveness as you and your witches are going to get, Géroux. Now, get out of my house."

"I'll take it." Mason rose to his feet, holding back a wince. His business was concluded; it was past time for him to return to Paradox. "And, for what it's worth, Rose and I, we are sorry for your loss."

CHAPTER 31
THE TALK

"You're wounded." Riding Hood knew wolves' bodies too well not to notice the discomfort he was trying to hide.

"It'll pass in a few days," Mason said as he ran his hands over the glass. The suspended animation chamber was on the way to Volumes & Vagaries. He had planned to go there and check in with Rose's sisters, but he couldn't bring himself to leave her side again. "And it was worth it. I still have the respect of the pack, and Preston's brother has agreed to let it go."

"The wondrous world of pack politics," she responded with a smile. "I've been on the wrong end of all that machismo and posturing a time or two myself. Can't say that I miss those days."

"It's not for everyone." Mason took no offense. "But there's more good than bad to it, at least, in *my* pack. Have Bluebell and the girls been able to figure anything out from the vial that might help Hyacinth?"

"They've been too busy hunting down answers for your Rose. There's no cure for the Macedonian nap yet, either, but they think the store's been trying to tell them the origin of her power. Even with Prisma's hand in it, the answer is unexpected."

Mason stared back at the tattooed woman expectantly. "And?'

"I can tell you if you'd like, Man Candy, but the little spitfire is going to be mad. Our redheaded resident Huxley made it clear she wanted to be the one. I don't suppose it makes any difference at this point, and her anger amuses me for some reason, so—it's Cronus."

"Who?"

"He's a Titan," Hood chuckled, "No wonder the bastard nuked the library."

"A Titan? That's impossible; the ancient gods faded—they just aren't that strong anymore."

"That's what we all thought, but, apparently, the ones that were stashed away in a maximum security prison didn't get the memo. Cronus's body might not be out and about, but your Rose is his furlough."

"From what little I remember of my mythology, he was the worst of them." Mason closed his eyes, taking a deep breath. It was unheard of, that kind of power—it certainly justified Rose's fears. "Killed his father or something like that; which is what I'd like to do to Prisma."

"Prisma's not a candidate for the Cronus technique. His parents were Uranus and Gaia; he castrated Uranus with a scythe and tossed his testicles into the sea. Later on, he ate his own children," Hood answered.

Mason's face paled beneath the dark, gray-dotted stubble. He was sharing Rose with a baby-eating, castration-happy god.

"You sure you want to go through with this mating bond thing? Your girl here might not be able to pop out pups, but there's still a lot of testosterone floating around in those big old wolf ba..."

"She's not Cronus," Mason said. He didn't want to think about it; especially not when they were having sex. "I trust Rose implicitly, with my heart *and* my balls. There's no one else for me. Once the bond is in place, we'll handle him together."

"I'm glad to hear you say that. If the girls can't find a way to negate the spell trapping her, then it's up to you to wake her."

"With a kiss, like the princes do in fairy tales?"

"Our sacred stories hold a clue," Riding Hood responded with a look that told him the fairy tale reference was a tad offensive, "but that crack-faced thing Ipos brought along with him was no joke. I can tell you right now, it's going to take more than a kiss to wake this one."

"A bite, then." Mason wasn't afraid; it was what he'd wanted all along.

"To start," Riding Hood said. "Don't forget, you need her to complete the mating bond. She has to claim you back if you hope to win for good."

"Win *what*? Once she's awake, she's awake."

"You might think so, but something tells me it's not going to be that easy. Rose might not be sleepwalking, but she has been sleeping, for a *while*, against her will."

Mason frowned. "You don't think she's the one in control in there. Is that why you've been by her side this whole time?"

"Bingo! Look at you, all brains and brawn—and here I thought all you were was easy on the eyes."

"Quit flirting; I already told you he's taken!" Iris, who had come out to give Riding Hood a break, insinuated herself between them. "And I thought I was going to be the one to break the news, hood girl."

"Yes," Hood responded dryly, "because you're such a peach with tact and diplomacy."

"Aww." Iris twirled a strand of red hair around one finger, turning it into flame. "You're starting to grow on me, too. Maybe later we can go to the mall together and get BFF tattoos—assuming there's room left anywhere on your slutty body."

"Iris," Mason sighed, "you really are being a bit..."

"What?" Iris batted her eyelashes at him. "Fabulous? Inspiring? Irreplaceable? Oh, I know, *irresistible*!"

"All of the above," Riding Hood said, giving the witch's back a heavy pat, "and, for the record, fire starter, every last mark on my body is magic. It's the blood of dragons, and each and every drop was freely given, straight from the vein. You have to *earn* this ink; it doesn't come from some collapsible mall kiosk outside the Metal memorabilia store."

"See you later, Dragon Ass!" Iris shouted as the tattooed woman left. She turned back to Mason with doe eyes, "Don't let her fool you; we've *really* started growing on each other. Like fungi."

"Do me a favor," Mason said, keeping his mouth shut about her antagonizing Hood. His ribs hurt, and he'd already fought enough battles for one day. "Get me one of those sleeping bags and a pillow, if you don't mind."

"Why? The ground is hard, and you look uncomfortable. You should come up to the loft and rest."

"No," Mason answered, "I've been away too long, and I'm not leaving Rose's side again."

CHAPTER 32
THE DREAM

"What *is* this place?" Prim looked down at her body and saw filthy rags. Thick chains bit into her ankles, and the door of a massive bronze gate shimmered in the distance, disappearing and reappearing in an eerie fog.

It all felt oddly familiar.

"The Desolation of Tartarus," a deep voice answered, echoing off the jagged edges of cave walls too far away to see.

"Is this Ipos's doing?"

She sank into the groove of a large rock behind her. There were five stones in total, each with a saddle-shaped pattern from supporting the weight of a colossal form over the ages.

"Rest easy, witch," the voice replied, "he's gone and couldn't reach you here, regardless. I am the only thing you need to fear between these walls. Even our brothers don't dare challenge me."

Primrose leaned back, looking up at where the sky should have been. If Ipos was gone, where was she? The stone pressed into her backside, filling her bones with an aching cold. There was nothing, just blackness churning above the fog. Now that she had seen it, she could feel its nothingness closing in.

"Brothers?" she pushed back her panic, counting the rocks again. Why had he said *our* brothers? It was a dream; a nightmare—it had to be.

"Family. You have four, then, like my sisters. What are their names?"

"We have five," the voice responded, rattling the ground. "Oceanus took no part in our war. You see the seats of Coeus, Crius, Hyperion, and Iapetus about you."

Prim looked around, her stomach growling with sudden hunger. She could feel herself shrinking and heard her skin rustling as it sunk in deep around her bones. She had just arrived here—how could she be starving?

"Those names ring a bell." She doubled over in pain. Her hair faded from yellow to white as her belly began to bloat.

"They should." Her bones shook along with the ground this time. Prim felt rattled and pained by the absolute strength of his voice.

"Why?" she rasped.

"We are the same, you and I; we are the first born, heirs to suffering and pain, both free and shackled. Your grandmother saw to that when she found a way to shove a contract—a loophole for *me*—through a portal. Even I still don't know how she managed it, and I doubt she does, either. She was pretty high, kept saying something about peyote."

"Gran?" Primrose realized she was talking with the thing inside of her. "Her bargain was a loophole?"

"Yes—a binding contract on indestructible Elysian paper, signed in both of our blood. So my brothers are yours, just as your sisters— Bluebell, Clover, Iris, and Hyacinth—are mine."

Primrose struggled to stand, alarmed at the sound of her sisters' names. Her legs failed, the muscles weak and atrophied. She dropped to the stone floor. *No*, this place couldn't be real; it wasn't *fair*. She had escaped Ipos, and she had Mason now; her life had become more than endless pain and suffering. She had to survive this and find a way back to him.

"I will *not* let you trap me in here," wracked with nausea, Primrose ground the words through her teeth, "and you will *not* hurt them."

"Such defiance in the face of defeat."

"You think this is defeat?" Prim crawled her way back to the rock. The muscles in her arms turned to gelatin. Patches of skin fell off them in white flakes that resembled snow as she pulled herself back to her feet. "I've got news for you; I'm going to kick your ass."

The resulting boom of laughter knocked her back down to her knees. Prim held back a sob from the jarring pain. She crawled back to the rock to repeat the process again. Her knees were scraped down to the cartilage and bone, and her hair was falling out.

She didn't care.

"Is that the best you've got?" A skeletal wreck, Primrose still taunted him. She balled her hands into fists to stop the shaking of her limbs. She would stay angry—she would *die* angry—before letting this thing win the contest of wills.

"Nowhere near it, little witch," he laughed even harder this time, "but that's all your going to get. Your body holds a piece of Tartarus, my prison; because it does, I could never hurt those for whom we care. You and I protected Hyacinth together that night. A part of you knows that—as it knows me. Tell me, Primrose, what is our name?"

Prim started to answer that he was crazy. She'd never heard his name before; how could she possibly know it? Then, something happened. The markings on her back tingled and pulsed; they heated her up from the inside, warming her against the chill. She felt her body healing, returning to its normal state.

With the healing, memories of things Primrose had never done— yet she had—flooded back to her. She stood before her brothers and a man who was a giant much like herself. They stripped his robes from him but left his sandals and his crown. A curved blade rested in her hand, its handle cold and smooth. She bent down while the others restrained him. The man, her father, struggled and screamed when she dug the scythe into his flesh—and then, the next memory came to her. She was eating her children on Mount Othrys.

Devouring them.

"No!" She screamed as the horrible images looped in her head. "Make it stop! I would never do those things!"

"But we did," the voice answered. "Your anger, the rage that compels you, has always been *mine*. You remember these things because you carry them inside of you. I have been a part of you from the moment of your conception, Primrose."

"This isn't real!"

"Your heart knows the truth; fighting me is useless. Find my name inside of you. Accept it and the visions end."

Tears rolled down her cheeks as she answered him, finally, "Cronus."

"Good girl."

Primrose sat back down. Her body shuddered; her bones crackled and popped. She was shrinking down to the size of a child's toy, a doll.

A hand gripped the back of Prim's tattered robe and lifted her; her feet dangled. She was helpless as a kitten while a dizzying mountain of muscle—thick legs, an abdomen, and chest—flew past her eyes.

"Will you devour me, too?" she cried.

"Relax, little witch." Cronus's breath ruffled her hair as he raised her higher still. "I've seen your world and that vainglorious demon opened you enough that I could finally show you mine. The worst is done; it's time we talk about a few things."

"I..." Primrose paused for a moment, overwhelmed.

She stared down at it all—past, present, and future—through a window in the dark eyes of Cronus, of herself: the god of Time.

CHAPTER 33
THE TEETH

"No!"

Mason bolted into a seated position. He scrambled out of the ridiculous anime sleeping bag Iris had given him with a disoriented growl and sniffed the air. Something had pulled him from his first decent sleep in quite a while. He looked up at the night sky of Paradox, whose constellations were always disturbingly out of order, then down at the figure under the glass.

He had heard her voice, and it hadn't been a part of his dream. Rose was still making noise as she slumbered—moaning and begging for someone to make it stop in there.

Make *what* stop?

His fingers traced frantically along the outside of the smooth glass as a chorus of annoyingly cheerful crickets serenaded him nearby. The box was seamless, with no handles anywhere on the damned thing. There had to be some way to release her—Hood had gotten Rose in there, after all. He picked up a landscaping rock from the side of a nearby building and raised it high over his head in a two-handed grip.

He brought the rock down forcefully. It bounced off thin air like a rubber ball before it could even hit the surface, yanking Mason's arms up along with it. All he got for his efforts was a dull ache in his healing rib; the chamber remained a frustrating enigma.

Mason was furious; something was happening to her in there.

Rose was restless, and it sounded as if she was suffering—what if it wasn't just a dream? He *had* to get her out.

After pacing and circling the box several more times, he tried running at the thing to ram it off its pedestal. The result was the same as the rock. Mason landed on the ground several feet away, with his head in his hands, cursing Paradox, and the Grays, and all their collective magic.

"I know you're only trying to protect Rose," he looked up at the sky and complained, "but, gods dammit, so am I; I *love* her!"

A star brightened above him, followed by a loud clap of thunder. The glass around Rose fell away at the sound, and the shards turned to lightning bugs before they hit the ground. All that was left was a white silk cushion and Rose, still wrapped up in the dream. The luminescent creatures zigged and zagged their way up into the heavens, eventually coming together to form a new star.

"You get brownie points for this," he said.

Though it was just a manner of expression, Mason couldn't help but wonder: Did the town have any brownies among the Gray? He could only recall meeting a sprite—the one Rose had hired to help out at Volumes & Vagaries.

"Rose." He leaned over her, smoothing a palm across her brow. "It's okay, love, I'm right here with you. Can you hear me, Rose? It's time to wake up and come back to me."

Primrose's lips moved; the voice that came from her was multi-layered and far too deep to be her own. *"Den eímaste echthroí; Eímaste éna."*

"I'm *not* going to lose you." Mason gripped her shoulders, shaking them. "Rose, wake up now; you need to snap out of this!"

"Den eímaste echthroí; Eímasteéna."

The words were louder this time. The force behind them shook the ground, lifting Rose's body from the pedestal. She remained there, levitating, as the stars twinkled above them. The edges of her hair hung down; a strand of it tickled Mason's arm.

"Listen to me, Cronus!" He loosened his grip when he realized it was leaving bruises on her skin. "Whatever you're doing in there—you cannot have her; she's *mine!*"

There was a rush of air, and Riding Hood appeared across from them in her nightgown. The iridescent ink she covered up with hoodies writhed and gleamed, the tattoos taking on a life of their own under the street lamps.

"Whoa, there!" Hood held her hands up in a sign of surrender as Mason whipped his head at her and snarled, his eyes turning gold. "It's just me. What's going on?"

Rose's eyes snapped open. The sockets were jet black, inked with the fabric of Time. Her head turned, and Cronus stared out at them.

"Den eímaste echthroí; Eímasteéna."

"What the hell is going on?" Mason looked into those dark eyes—eyes that were disturbingly unfamiliar—and refused to let go. "Rose?"

"That's a shitty answer, hood girl," Iris said, jogging up in her purple and black striped pajamas, with Clover and Blue close behind her in robes.

"Nice tats," Clover told Hood. "What's Mason doing to Prim?"

"That's not Mason's doing." Bluebell rubbed her Baby Huxley bump, cocking her head back at the dark eyes that considered her intently. "He's not hurting her, either; he's just in control."

"If someone's in control," Clover responded dryly, "then we're obviously not talking about Mason."

"You're not helping." Mason never took his eyes off Rose.

"She's not because she can't," Hood said. "Remember our conversation, Wolf—I think it's time; you need to wake her up."

"But we don't have a way to negate the spell yet," Bluebell said.

"He doesn't need it." Hood was confident.

"Let me guess." Clover sounded skeptical. "He's got love."

"And great big…"

"Balls!" Iris shouted.

Mason glared at her—his canines lengthened, and his eyes blazed. She backed up a step in the street, bumping into Clover.

"Teeth," Riding Hood said with a look of warning. It was not the time for childish games, not if they wanted Primrose back in control of her own body.

"You think the mating bond will bring her back to us?" Bluebell asked.

"I do," Hood said. "I've seen its power."

"Hold on a minute," Iris responded. "Don't they have to get it on to seal the mating part of that deal?"

"Yes."

"In the *street?*"

"If you start singing The Beatles, I'm going to kill you," Clover said.

"What?" Iris looked at her.

"Oh, come on—'Why Don't We Do It In the Road?'—I know you know the words."

"Oh, yeah!" Iris immediately dove into an off-key rendition. "Why don't we..."

"Shut it," Blue said when Mason growled at them, "both of you. *Right* now."

"Don't worry," Riding Hood watched as he lowered his head to Primrose's neck. "Although I'd love to see what kind of wedding tackle Mr. Man Candy over here is sporting, there's no need to—once his bite pulls her out of it, we're leaving them alone."

CHAPTER 34
THE AWAKENING

Primrose was adrift, floating through corridors past abstract paintings, wooden mantles ablaze with candles, and open doors. The corridors were passages of time in a continuum, something she had been able to access through the eyes of Cronus. Iris would have geeked out over it in a nanosecond, but Prim had never been all that big on sci-fi, and she had an agenda, so she wasn't hyper-focusing.

Somewhere out there, waiting for her to find it, was the point in time where the original Huxley curse began. If she could see how the sorcerers made it, and what the wicked queen had made them do, maybe she could find a way to right things for her sisters. Cronus had already warned her. Free diving through a time stream was dangerous, and he couldn't give her access to all of his powers to help because they might destroy her.

She told him she understood, but she might never have the opportunity again.

A yellow door coated with flowers grabbed her attention; she floated through it into a room filled with scenes from her childhood. Bits and pieces of her and her sisters' memories flew by—diving into a lake together, learning spells, and watching their mother go insane.

She turned a corner and found her mother, Calla. She saw the gaunt, hollow-eyed madness they all remembered. Then, she saw Calla at a point before the insanity had overtaken her. At twenty-five, Calla Huxley had been a starry-eyed witch in love with a dangerous man. Life and hope filled her eyes, despite all of Prisma's dire warnings. *You can never marry; you'll never have true love, girl; it's not in the cards.*

"Rose, it's okay, love; I'm right here with you!" Mason's voice called out to her. "Can you hear me, Rose? It's time to wake up and come back to me!"

Next, there was Prisma's life; it was twisted and ambitious, yes, but also filled with unexpected love. Primrose saw the real reason Prisma had finally murdered Calla's husband, her father—the man had been evil. And she saw how Gran had fallen for a human, Calla's father, long before the locket existed. He died from a plague, leaving her pregnant before they could marry.

"I'm not going to lose you!" The sound of Mason's voice grew faint, but, surely, she didn't have far to go. "Rose, wake up now! You need to snap out of this!"

Prim drifted deeper, past the lives of more ancestral witches. She witnessed their hearts systematically broken; the love was invariably stripped away from them—sometimes through pride or deceit, often tragedy.

Numbness seeped into her limbs as she progressed. The candles down the corridor dimmed and sputtered. A feeling of abandonment washed over her—the more she persisted, the more the continuum fought her.

"Rose?"

Prim looked down at her palms in horror. The fingers of her right hand dissolved into dust, floating away into the encroaching blackness.

She tried to scream—send her *back*; she wanted to go *back*—but had no vocal cords to make the sound.

Time was erasing her.

Suddenly, a sharp pain—a beautiful, excruciating feeling—pulled Prim back together and reeled her in. Slammed back into her body, locked in place, her consciousness struggled momentarily, desperate to reorient itself in the darkness.

There were teeth in her shoulder.

"Mason." Primrose breathed in the scent of him, holding on tightly as Cronus receded and her levitation came to an end.

The inkiness in her eyes retreated, restoring her vision. Prim was outside in the road; her sisters—all but Hyacinth—and Riding Hood were there. And Paradox's stars twinkled in the sky, high above them.

"Rose," Mason said, raising his head. His voice was gruff as he laid her back onto the cushion on the pedestal. "I thought I'd lost you."

Primrose reached up to take his face between her hands. She winced in pain from the shoulder muscle that suffered through his deep bite. A smile crossed her face. Of all of her scars, this was the only one she would never mind bearing. It was definitive proof that they belonged together, and *no one* could deny it.

"You saved me," she told him, her voice hoarse.

"And you didn't even try to kill me *once*," he teased. Mason added, a bit more seriously, "I claimed you, you know; you're mine for good. I hope you're not angry, Rose."

Tendrils of magic curled from her fingertips, wrapping around Mason's head. They shot down his neck and torso, racing for his toes and back up again. Primrose bathed him in warmth and glowing light—in the manifestation of her power and love.

She cleared her throat and spoke a bit louder, her voice returning to normal, "And now I've claimed you, too."

"Nice!" Iris fidgeted as the magic receded beneath Mason's skin. The ADD she swore she didn't have was kicking in again. "Hey! Do you think we could get her to do that again at Christmastime?"

"Don't make me punch you," Clover said.

"Guys!" Blue nodded at Mason and Primrose as they turned to stare back at the group expectantly.

"Got it," Riding Hood responded. Mason fiddled with the buttons on his shirt. She wondered if Primrose had topped off the healing of his rib. Even if it hadn't, something told her Mason didn't care. "It's sexy time; let's get out of here, ladies."

CHAPTER 35
THE SURPRISE

"So you don't believe Cronus did it on purpose? What does Mason have to say about it?" Blue threaded a fancy string through the last of the laddered holes on the back of Prim's dress thoughtfully.

"Cronus and I talked about it," Primrose responded with a shrug. A handful of long corkscrew curls cascaded over one shoulder, bouncing in time with the motion. "Taking over was just his way of acting as a place marker for my body. None of it was his fault; he warned me it was dangerous, going that far back in the time stream."

"But you almost faded away—just like the gods did—and Cronus did nothing to save you. *Mason* had to bring you back, Prim."

"I know, Blue: I was there. Either way, I'm telling you, I still believe Cronus. Mason's not sure yet; he's reserving judgment."

"Your body is part of some weird timeshare with a deity now—that's a bit hard for *all* of us to handle."

Primrose stared at her reflection in the mirror. The lips moved whenever she spoke, sure, but was that *really* her? She had never envisioned herself wearing a wedding gown or preparing to walk down the aisle.

"He's been inside of me since I was born, Blue."

The white dress the Council had not just provided but also insisted she wear—a means of apology to the only resident now hosting a god—was incredible. It was a 12th-century patterned gown, with trailing sleeves, a layered skirt, and a long gold braided belt for the handfasting ritual.

"Alright, Prim; point taken."

Aspects of the dress had a modern adaptation. Crafted from soft, local silk, it had a V-shaped neck that showed enough collarbone and cleavage to make a friar faint. And the lace scraps Riding Hood had picked out for her to wear underneath it were downright indecent. Nevertheless, the period gown was an acknowledgment of the way things should have always been; it was the symbolic erasing of a bond with a false bride, one that had caused so much unnecessary pain.

"You're the prettiest thing ever, Primrose Huxley!" Iris appeared behind her in the mirror. She set a bouquet of red and white roses threaded with gold ribbons on a table by the door.

"Yeah." Clover smiled at her. "Ditto what Sparky said."

Primrose laughed, shaking her head. "Don't go getting so excited; it's still just your sister under all this fancy wrapping paper. Has anybody seen Hyacinth yet?"

"Not yet," Clover responded, "but she swore Ipos was letting her come with an escort since Paradox is refusing him reentrance."

"I hope he's not lying," Primrose wasn't exactly trustful of the newer, gentler Hyacinth-loving demon. Obviously, neither was Paradox "I need to talk to her in person and make sure she's okay; I hate that she got roped into Gran's plans for saving me."

"At least, you know Gran cares," Clover said, glaring at Iris—a warning not to start with any negative, anti-Prisma crap on Prim's wedding day. "I've only been trying to tell you that forever."

"Zip it!" Iris responded. "This is a wedding that's about to go down, not a Granapalooza Love Fest sing-along. And you're still a horrible judge of character, you Succubus lo…"

A blast of wind knocked Iris into the wall. She arose with flames shooting out of her fingertips. Blue shook her head no, pointing to the doorway, and the two exited, whispering heatedly at one another.

"They'd tear down the building if we let them," Blue said, pulling Prim to her feet and handing her the bouquet. "We can't let anyone ruin the magic of this day for you."

"Wisely spoken," a voice answered from the corridor, over the tranquil sounds of a harp's music drifting by from the main room.

"Hello, Gran." Primrose turned to look at the brunette in the elegantly understated pants suit stepping out of an unsanctioned portal. Her hazel eyes were much like Prim's, minus the red. "I've been expecting you. It's alright, Blue—you can leave us now."

"You expected me, hm? You know, if I hadn't driven your mother insane, she would be here instead." Prisma circled Prim as Bluebell left them, taking in the hair and the dress. "It looks like they did you justice, child."

"More than anyone ever has you" Primrose said, taking both of her grandmother's hands. The digits were soft and unlined, the same as hers. "I've seen the truth, and you're not who I thought you were."

"So, you and Cronus have come to terms, then."

"In a manner of speaking," she answered. "I can't approve of what you've done to Cyn, but I'm glad you've come."

"She'll be okay, and I haven't come for your approval. The day you approve of a wicked old witch like *me*," Prisma remarked, taking her by the crook of the arm with a warm smile, "is the day we're all lost."

"Why *did* you come?"

"To give you away to that good-looking wolf in the expensive tuxedo out there."

"What about my sisters?"

"It's not their wedding day."

"Borana?"

"She's where she needs to be."

"You're using her for something, aren't you?"

"*Hush*," Prisma said, placing a finger on the button of Prim's nose, just as she had when Prim was small, "and heed your sister's advice. Don't let anything ruin the magic. You've fought hard to earn this moment, young witch—worry has no power in your world, not for today."

CHAPTER 36
THE WEDDING

"I can't believe the whole pack is here," Prim said, peering around the corner at the nerve-racking crowd in the Main Hall, "even Preston's sister."

"It would be disrespectful *not* to come," Prisma responded matter-of-factly, straightening the folds of Primroses's gown, "and you need to get used to them. You're marrying an Alpha; that makes you one, too."

"Look! It's Hyacinth." Primrose nodded at the two figures just arriving.

Cyn wore a blue muslin gown and elegant shawl, with a matching ribbon covering the scar on her throat; she looked just like a Princess. After brief eye contact with Prim and Prisma, she and her escort headed their way.

"I was worried Ipos lied about letting her come."

"He's a tricky one," Prisma said, "but Hyacinth can handle him. She's not the wilting flower you all think she is. Who's the two-headed goon in the suit with her? Is he layering a t-shirt underneath there?"

"That's magic-proof security detail to make sure we don't try and steal her back. His name is Cyril."

"Well, he's certainly a big boy, isn't he? Santino looks none too happy about him making googly eyes at Iris, either."

"Yeah," Prim admitted with a laugh, "We think Cyril's sweet on her. He finds Iris's insults hilarious, and it looks like they share the same fashion sense. You never know; a little competition might be just the thing to push Santino out of his comfort zone in BFF territory."

"BFF?"

"Best friends forever," Primrose replied, signaling for silence as the two came closer.

"Prim!" Hyacinth glanced at their grandmother, and then beamed at the bride. "Look at you; you're an angel!"

"A badly tarnished one with red eyes," Primrose joked.

The color didn't bother her anymore; if Mason accepted everything she was, so could she. That was why she had gone with a crown of flowers, instead of the traditional veil—no more hiding.

After a minor hiccup or two, Prim was adjusting decently to a life without spectacles. Cronus had explained a bit more about how the dimensional aspect of her vision worked, and he was teaching her how to control it. Until she decided it was time to look for anything useful—a clue to the true nature of something, or a glimpse of its future or past—all she would see were auras.

"You wouldn't want to be an angel," Cyril felt obligated to say something, "most of them are so innocent it comes off as stupid."

"I'm not likely to argue with you," Prisma said, looking at her youngest granddaughter. "You are positively *radiant*, Hyacinth. Tell me; how is life with Ipos treating you?"

"Wonderfully," Hyacinth answered, "although I had to chat with his kitchen staff about the contents of a proper meal. Luckily, they seem to like me. Now, it's nothing but gourmet everything and closets full of clothes, more than I could ever wear. It's like I'm his personal Barbie doll—and he even does yoga with me in the evenings, now."

"Funny." Prisma wasn't in the least surprised that her love spell appeared to be working wonders for the girl. "I got the impression he thought dolls were ... let me see; how did he put it? Creepy."

"Not this one." Cyril rolled his eyes, jerking a thumb in Hyacinth's direction.

"Then everything is as it should be. Cyril, you and I are going to let the girls have their warm, fuzzy moment in peace. Then, you're going to take Hyacinth back out there. Her sister and I need to get this show down the aisle."

After several hugs, a brief discussion of Cronus, Ipos, rediscovering Cyn's powers, and yoga, Hyacinth left. There might have also been a delicately posed question on the wisdom of trusting Gran not to foul up the wedding.

Primrose finally emerged on her grandmother's arm at the back of the hall, with butterflies and rabid squirrels in her stomach. Until that moment, she had no idea how hard it could be, just concentrating on putting one foot in front of the other and not sweating. Riding Hood sang a lovely duet with Reemy—he wore a cast on one leg but was recovering well—as the elder Huxley escorted her down the aisle.

"Now," Prisma said and squeezed her arm as they closed the distance between Prim and the broad-shouldered Alpha at the end of the enchanted red carpet. Mason looked fantastic in a steel colored suit, crisp white shirt, and bowtie. He stared back at Primrose as if he'd never, in his entire life, beheld a more beautiful sight. "*That* is a man worth waiting centuries for."

Primrose smiled at Mason's surprise when she whispered an introduction. Prisma mentioned something about it being a pleasure, and not overstaying her welcome, and then she vanished with a wink.

"Well," Mrs. Grimm said, nodding at Bluebell, "let's steal the spotlight back, shall we?"

Blue waved her hands above her head in a scattering motion and said four words: "*Avium petalis. Caelo revelatum.*" A large, circular portion of the roof blew away to reveal the crystal blue sky of a warm Paradox afternoon. An army of fragrant petals floated in through the hole. They came to rest in a lovely canopy several feet above the heads of the bride and groom.

"Friends, family, and members of Council prone to making nasty phone calls," Mrs. Grimm announced, eyeing a few faces in the crowd with displeasure, "we are all gathered here today to witness and celebrate the union of Primrose Huxley and Mason Géroux. If you have any objections, kindly keep them to yourselves, or leave now, before you suffer grievous injury."

Satisfied there were no protests, or subsequent deaths to go on record, Mrs. Grimm consecrated a circle of carpet around the couple. She called on the powers of the East, South, West, and the North to bless Mason and Prim and their marriage. A hush fell over the crowd—seriously, even Iris shut up—and the ceremony started.

"We begin with the binding of hands," Mrs. Grimm said and winked at the two of them, "symbolic of the joining of this couple."

Prim's belt untied, the long gold rope hovering in the air between her and Mason. She searched his eyes, making sure he was still on board.

Restraints were not something a wolf handled easily; they had discussed it in detail. He wanted to do this for her—a small gesture, a surrender of his own, after all of the things she had gone through.

"You're not getting out of it that easily, Rose." Mason smiled, his eyes glowing gold as he took her hands in his own. "I play for keeps, remember?"

The gold fabric looped their hands, leaving space for circulation but clinging tightly enough to bind them. Someone coughed in the audience—probably Iris or Cyril—then Mrs. Grimm asked Mason and Prim six questions. They responded to each with "I will."

The vows and rings came next; the rope unwound and returned itself neatly to Prim's waist. She and Mason had decided to keep their words short and straightforward. Primrose still wasn't big on crowds, and they had the rest of forever to tell each other what, and how, they felt.

"I," Primrose said, with tears in her eyes (although she swore it wouldn't happen), "choose you, Mason Géroux, to stand by and sleep with, to champion fiercely and love, through whatever may come, for the rest of our immortal days."

"And I," Mason reminded himself that Alpha's didn't cry, "choose you, Primrose Huxley, to stand by and sleep with, to champion fiercely and love, through whatever may come, for the rest of our immortal days."

"Mason and Primrose, on behalf of all these witnesses, and by the strength of your love, I pronounce you two married. Kiss away!"

The shower of rose petals fell in a circle, scattering onto the red fabric around them and melting seamlessly into it. Primrose placed her hands on Mason's shoulders and said one word.

"Finally."

Bluebell clapped her hands together, along with the crowd. She and Mrs. Grimm shared a glance as she thought back to their earlier conversation about her vision.

Using the flowers made sense. The petals hadn't been an awful omen at all. They were a symbol of Prim's old life, of her fear and loneliness. Mason had to pluck that all away from her to give her a new one filled with happiness and love.

Afterward, the girls gathered briefly to discuss the future. Hyacinth would go back to Ipos of her own free will. The pack would stay and build housing in Paradox; Riding Hood was elated to learn how many of them were single. And Clover would hang out and run the store while Prim and Mason honeymooned.

The newlyweds had chosen somewhere peaceful—a remote cabin nestled in the mountains of Southern California. It was just outside the town of Big Bear. Mason's pack had done favors for a few bear shifters there over the years, and their Alpha was more than happy to welcome him and his bride to their territory for a little R & R.

Once they got back, Primrose was going to be busy, as Iris put it, "learning all that boss lady, Queen Bitch Alpha stuff." Clover said she was willing to hang out indefinitely, and, hopefully, forget about her broken heart. And Iris planned to stay with Blue for support while they hunted down Super Baby Huxley's deadbeat daddy.

Cyril agreed to Hyacinth's request to keep the demonic head honcho in the dark. In return, she would tell him all about Iris. He had high hopes of wooing the redhead away from the tall, pale Santino.

EPILOGUE

"*That's* why you should let me go," Borana added decisively, finishing off her tea.

Sure, she was already pissed off at her companions' complete inability to compromise, but that didn't mean she would ever stop trying. Especially not after hearing the news about Clover staying on in Paradox to heal a broken heart.

"Trust me," Prisma said, reaching back to stroke the head of the large black cat that had launched itself onto her shoulder, "your part in Primrose's battle was through when we brought you back."

"No, it *wasn't*! I know Ipos; there's bound to be more trouble coming, and I'm an extra hand in the fight! I can still help them."

"That's your ego talking, dear—you just want Clover to see whose side you are on so that she'll forgive you. None of that changes the fact that King returned."

"He's just a cat. You can't seriously tell me that you decide the outcome of significant events based on..."

"Better not to question these things," the tree interrupted. "King has a ninety-nine percent accuracy rate—that's better than any god or government—and we need to prepare you for succession."

"Listen," Borana argued, "I'm as big a fan of pussy as the next gal—probably, more so—but a cat with creepy eyes coming home is not a good enough sign."

The cat licked at one of his padded feet, chewing a claw

momentarily before rolling his blue eyes and answering in an Irish lilt, "And if it were a talking cat, oh ye of little faith?"

Borana blinked. "You talk?"

"I just did." The cat blinked back. "Actually and factually; no faith required, lass—are you simple-minded? Why would you even *ask* that question?"

"I don't think her mind is simple." The tree Borana knew as Conifer defended her. "She seems sharp to me. She's probably just in shock."

"No, look at her," King spoke, his whiskers quivering indignantly, "she's a demon—from *Hell!* They have far more shocking things than talking cats. Therefore, I call the basis of your argument invalid, Conjure."

"Conjure?" Borana looked at Prisma for help. "I thought she said her name was Coni..."

"I'm the Inn, sweetheart," the tree said, looking alarmed.

"Scratch that," the cat responded, swiping a paw in the air. "I amend my prior commentary: The Succubus isn't simple-minded. She's sex-addled and mentally bankrupt. Guilty of a negative IQ score; not an ounce of water left in the fishbowl, I tell you!"

"I thought you would have figured it out by now," Conifer mumbled, shaking her leaves in distress. "Who I am, you know, based on the job interview."

"Enough!" Prisma clapped her hands authoritatively. "Borana isn't stupid—sex rarely makes *women* stupid—and I'm still getting out of here; got it?"

"Fine."

"Alright."

"I guess so."

"Good!" the witch replied, leading their odd party into the maze.

"I hope they're going to be alright without me," Borana sighed. "Not just Clover and Primrose, but Hyacinth and the others, too. Ipos is such a beast."

"A beast in love," King said.

"Yes, in *love*," Conjure echoed, "which makes him an entirely different thing."

"You were only useful to them because of me," Prisma commented, patting Borana on the shoulder. "Don't look so *sad*; your Auntie Golem says she's coming to stay with you."

"That's good," Borana said, "but I don't want her—I want *Clover*."

"That's not very nice," King said.

"Nothing's ever really over." Conifer tried to be helpful. "Think of this as merely a sabbatical from the girls and their troubles. You need to learn the ropes—*my* ropes—if you wish to be highly effective. You must pick me up like a habit and hang on tight, dear."

"The Conjure Inn has always been a valuable asset and ally to its partners," Prisma agreed. "And she's right, Borana, your role in my granddaughters' saga is *hardly* through."

"Chin up, Dum-Dum," King said as he launched off the witch's shoulders and onto his feet, stretching his legs. "It's the truth, so there's no need to dawdle. The wicked old witchy-poo here might lie to you, but I wouldn't. Frankly, there's no point in wasting the energy when I don't like you."

"I like you *better* when you're quiet." Borana followed the cat's tail around the corner into an area that was unlike anything she had ever seen before.

"That's because your mind is still too small, boring Borana. And the sooner we expand the peanut you've been lugging around in there, the better off we'll *all* be."

"Where are we?" she asked, too surprised to take insult.

"Everywhere and nowhere, dear" Prisma answered as the world shifted sideways around them, "the perfect place for us to start!"

"Exactly!" King's smile broke apart into sunlight, dancing all around them as the sound of his laughter echoed in the air.

ABOUT THE AUTHOR

Jennifer / J. A. Fales is an award-winning author, freelance writer, and Southern California resident. She loves travel and people watching, and considers herself a foodie and a wine enthusiast. Her twitter handle is @JenniferFalesCA and the web address for her blog is http://perhapslucidity.com.